BABY DOLL & TIGEF

By TENNESSEE WILLIAMS

PLAYS

Baby Doll & Tiger Tail
Camino Real
Cat on a Hot Tin Roof
Clothes for a Summer Hotel
Dragon Country
The Glass Menagerie
A Lovely Sunday for Creve Coeur
The Red Devil Battery Sign
Small Craft Warnings
Stopped Rocking and Other Screenplays
A Streetcar Named Desire
Sweet Bird of Youth
THE THEATRE OF TENNESSEE WILLIAMS, VOLUME I
  Battle of Angels, A Streetcar Named Desire, The Glass Menagerie
THE THEATRE OF TENNESSEE WILLIAMS, VOLUME II
  *The Eccentricities of a Nightingale, Summer and Smoke, The Rose
  Tattoo, Camino Real*
THE THEATRE OF TENNESSEE WILLIAMS, VOLUME III
  Cat on a Hot Tin Roof, Orpheus Descending, Suddenly Last Summer
THE THEATRE OF TENNESSEE WILLIAMS, VOLUME IV
  Sweet Bird of Youth, Period of Adjustment, The Night of the Iguana
THE THEATRE OF TENNESSEE WILLIAMS, VOLUME V
  *The Milk Train Doesn't Stop Here Anymore, Kingdom of Earth (The Seven
  Descents of Myrtle), Small Craft Warnings, The Two-Character Play*
THE THEATRE OF TENNESSEE WILLIAMS, VOLUME VI
  27 Wagons Full of Cotton and Other Short Plays
THE THEATRE OF TENNESSEE WILLIAMS, VOLUME VII
  In the Bar of a Tokyo Hotel and Other Plays
27 Wagons Full of Cotton and Other Plays
The Two-Character Play
Vieux Carré

POETRY

Androgyne, Mon Amour
In the Winter of Cities

PROSE

Collected Stories
Eight Mortal Ladies Possessed
Hard Candy and Other Stories
One Arm and Other Stories
The Roman Spring of Mrs. Stone
Where I Live: Selected Essays

BABY DOLL
& TIGER TAIL

A SCREENPLAY AND PLAY by

TENNESSEE
WILLIAMS

A NEW DIRECTIONS BOOK

Manufactured in the United States of America
New Directions Books are printed on acid-free paper.
First published clothbound and as New Directions Paperbook 714 in 1991.
Published simultaneously in Canada by Penguin Books Canada Limited.

Library of Congress Cataloging-in-Publication Data

Williams, Tennessee, 1911–1983.
    Baby doll & tiger tail : a screenplay and play / by Tennessee Williams.
    p.   cm.
    ISBN 0–8112–1166–5 (alk. paper) : $23.95. — ISBN 0–8112–1167–3
(pbk. : alk. paper) : $11.95
    I. Title.   II. Title: Baby doll and tiger tail.
PS3545.I5365B29   1991
812'.54—dc20   91–6848
                                                                    CIP

New Directions Books are published for James Laughlin
by New Directions Publishing Corporation,
80 Eighth Avenue, New York 10011
SECOND PRINTING

BABY DOLL

PRINCIPAL CHARACTERS
(in order of appearance)

BABY DOLL MEIGHAN
ARCHIE LEE MEIGHAN
AUNT ROSE COMFORT McCORKLE
OLD FUSSY, *a chicken*
BARTENDER
MAC
THE OLD BOY
SILVA VACARRO
ROCK
A MAN
MARSHAL
NEGRO BOY
CLERK
MOOSE

From the PUBLISHER'S NOTE to the
1956 Edition of *Baby Doll*

For a number of years Elia Kazan, the director of several of Tennessee Williams' plays on Broadway as well as films, had been urging Mr. Williams to weld into an original film story two of his early one-act plays ["27 Wagons Full of Cotton," and "The Long Stay Cut Short or The Unsatisfactory Supper"] which were, roughly, concerned with the same characters and situation. And in the summer of 1955, while he was traveling in Europe, Mr. Williams wrote and dispatched to Mr. Kazan a proposed script, quite different from the two short plays. With some changes this was filmed the following winter mainly in the Mississippi rural area which had been the original setting of the two short plays.

Although he had himself adapted several of his Broadway successes for films, this was Mr. Williams' first original screen play. Many who came to read it, including his publishers, felt that although few "shooting" scripts have ever been published, this one was publishable as it stood. . . .

The film, *Baby Doll*, which was previously announced as *The Whip Hand* and *Mississippi Woman*, was produced and directed in the winter of 1955–1956 by Elia Kazan for Newtown Productions, Inc., and is released by Warner Brothers. The principal roles are filled by Carroll Baker, Eli Wallach, Karl Malden and Mildred Dunnock.

BABY DOLL

1] INTERIOR. DAY.

A voluptuous girl, under twenty, is asleep on a bed, with the covers thrown off. This is Baby Doll Meighan, Archie Lee's virgin wife. A sound is disturbing her sleep, a steady sound, furtive as a mouse scratching, she stirs, it stops, she settles again, it starts again. Then she wakes, without moving, her back to that part of the wall from which the sound comes.

2] INTERIOR. DAY. CLOSE SHOT. BABY DOLL.

She is a little frightened of what sounds like a mouse in the woodwork and still doesn't sound like a mouse in the woodwork. Then a crafty look.

3] INTERIOR. DAY. FULL SHOT.

She gets up, as the sound is continuing, and moves stealthily out of her room.

4] HALL. DAY. FULL SHOT.

She comes out of her room and just as stealthily opens the door to an adjoining room and peeks in.

5] CLOSE SHOT. BABY DOLL.

Astonished and angry at what she sees.

6] WHAT SHE SEES. ARCHIE LEE MEIGHAN.

He is crouched over a section of broken plaster in the wall, enlarging a space between exposed boards with a penknife. Unshaven, black jowled, in sweaty pajamas. On the bed table behind him is a half-empty bottle of liquor, an old alarm clock, ticking away, a magazine called Spicy Fiction *and a tube of ointment. After a moment he removes the knife and bends to peer through the enlarged crack.*

5

7] CLOSE SHOT. BABY DOLL.

BABY DOLL: Archie Lee. You're a mess.

8] ARCHIE LEE.
He recovers.

9] BABY DOLL.

BABY DOLL: Y'know what they call such people? Peepin' Toms!

10] FULL SHOT. ARCHIE LEE'S BEDROOM.

ARCHIE: Come in here, I want to talk to you.

BABY DOLL: I know what you're going to say, but you can save your breath.

ARCHIE [*interrupting*]: We made an agreement . . .

BABY DOLL: You promised my daddy that you would leave me alone till I was ready for marriage. . . .

ARCHIE: Well?

BABY DOLL: Well, I'm not ready for it yet. . . .

ARCHIE: And I'm going crazy. . . .

BABY DOLL: Well, you can just wait. . . .

ARCHIE: We made an agreement that when you was twenty years old we could be man and wife in more than just in name only.

BABY DOLL: Well, I won't be twenty till November the seventh. . . .

6

ARCHIE: Which is the day after tomorrow!

BABY DOLL: How about your side of that agreement—that you'd take good care of me? GOOD CARE OF ME! Do you remember that?! Now the Ideal Pay As You Go Plan Furniture Company is threatening to remove the furniture from this house. And every time I bring that up you walk away. . . .

ARCHIE: Just going to the window to get a breath of air. . . .

BABY DOLL: Now I'm telling you that if the Ideal Pay As You Go Plan Furniture Company takes those five complete sets of furniture out of this house then the understanding between us will be canceled. Completely!

11] ARCHIE LEE. AT WINDOW.
He is listening. We hear the distant sound of the Syndicate Cotton Gin. Like a gigantic distant throbbing heartbeat. Archie Lee puts the window down. He crosses to the mirror, dolefulllly considers his appearance.

BABY DOLL: Yeah, just look at yourself! You're not exactly a young girl's dream come true, Archie Lee Meighan.

[*The phone rings downstairs. This sound is instantly followed by an outcry even higher and shriller.*]

BABY DOLL: Aunt Rose Comfort screams ev'ry time the phone rings.

ARCHIE: What does she do a damn fool thing like that for?

[*The phone rings again. Aunt Rose Comfort screams downstairs. The scream is followed by high breathless laughter. These sounds are downstairs. Archie Lee exits.*]

BABY DOLL: She says a phone ringing scares her.

7

12] HALL.
[*Archie lumbers over to a staircase, much too grand for the present style of the house, and shouts down to the old woman below.*]

ARCHIE: Aunt Rose Comfort, why don't you answer that phone?

13] DOWNSTAIRS HALL.
[*Aunt Rose comes out of the kitchen and walks towards the hall telephone, withered hand to her breast.*]

AUNT ROSE: I cain't catch m'breath, Archie Lee. Phone give me such a fright.

ARCHIE [*from above*]: Answer it.

[*She has recovered some now and gingerly lifts the reciever.*]

AUNT ROSE: Hello? This is Miss Rose Comfort McCorkle speaking. No, the lady of the house is Mrs. Archie Lee Meighan, who is the daughter of my brother that passed away . . .

[*Archie Lee is hurrying down the stairs.*]

ARCHIE: They don't wanta know that! Who in hell is it talking and what do they want?

AUNT ROSE: I'm hard of hearing. Could you speak louder, please? The what? The Ideal Pay As—

[*With amazing, if elephantine, speed, Archie snatches the phone from the old woman.*]

ARCHIE: Gi'me that damn phone. An' close the door.

8

[*The old woman utters her breathless cackle and backs against the door. Archie speaks in a hoarse whisper.*]

ARCHIE: Now what is this? Aw. Uh-huh. Today!? Aw. You gotta g'me more time. Yeah, well you see I had a terrible setback in business lately. The Syndicate Plantation built their own cotton gin and're ginnin' out their own cotton, now, so I lost their trade and it's gonna take me a while to recover from that. . . .

[*Suddenly.*]

Then TAKE IT OUT! TAKE IT OUT! Come and get th' damn stuff. And you'll never get my business again! Never!

[*They have hung up on him. He stands there—a man in tough trouble. Then abruptly starts massaging his exhausted head of hair.*]

AUNT ROSE [*timidly*]: Archie Lee, honey, you all aren't going to lose your furniture, are you?

ARCHIE [*hoarse whisper*]: Will you shut up and git on back in the kitchen and don't speak a word that you heard on the phone, if you heard a word, to my wife! And don't holler no more in this house, and don't cackle no more in it either, or by God I'll pack you up and haul you off to th' county home at Sunset.

AUNT ROSE: What did you say, Archie Lee, did you say something to me?

ARCHIE: Yeah, I said shoot.

[*He starts upstairs. Aunt Rose cackles uneasily and enters the kitchen. Suddenly, we hear another scream from her. We pan with her, and reveal Old Fussy, the hen, on top of the kitchen table pecking the corn bread.*]

9

14] UPSTAIRS HALL.

Archie is heading back to his bedroom. Baby Doll appears in a flimsy wrapper at the turn of the stairs crossing to the bathroom.

BABY DOLL: What made her holler this time?

ARCHIE: How in hell would I know what made that ole woman holler this time or last time or the next time she hollers.

BABY DOLL: Last time she'hollered it was because you throwed something at her.

[*She enters bathroom. Archie Lee stands in doorway.*]

ARCHIE: What did I ever throw at Aunt Rose Comfort?

BABY DOLL [*from inside bathroom*]: Glass a water. Fo' singin' church hymns in the kitchen. . . .

[*We hear the shower go on.*]

ARCHIE: This much water! Barely sprinkled her with it! To catch her attention. She don't hear nothing, you gotta do somethin' to git the ole woman's attention.

[*On an abrupt impulse he suddenly enters the bathroom. Sounds of a struggle. The shower.*]

BABY DOLL: Keep y'r hands off me! Will yuh? Keep your hands off . . . Off.

[*Archie Lee comes out of the bathroom good and wet. The shower is turned off. Baby Doll's head comes out past the door.*]

BABY DOLL: I'm going to move to the Kotton King Hotel, the very next time you try to break the agreement! The very next time!

10

[*She disappears.* . . .]

15] CLOSE SHOT. ARCHIE LEE WET. DISSOLVE.

16] ARCHIE LEE.
He is seated in his 1937 Chevy Sedan. The car is caked with pale brown mud and much dented. Pasted on the windshield is a photo of Baby Doll smiling with bewilderment at the birdie-in-the-camera. Archie Lee is honking his horn with unconcealed and unmodified impatience.

ARCHIE [*shouting*]: Baby Doll! Come on down here, if you're going into town with me. I got to be at the doctor's in ten minutes. [*No answer.*] Baby Doll!!!

[*From inside the house. Baby Doll's voice.*]

BABY DOLL: If you are so impatient, just go ahead without me. Just go ahead. I know plenty of ways of getting downtown without you.

ARCHIE: You come on.

[*Silence. The sound of the Syndicate Gin. Archie does a sort of imitation. His face is violent.*]

ARCHIE: Baby Doll!!!

[*Baby Doll comes out on the sagging porch of the mansion. She walks across the loose boards of the porch through stripes of alternate light and shadow from the big porch pillars. She is humming a little cakewalk tune, and she moves in sympathy to it. She has on a skirt and blouse, white, and skintight, and pearl chokers the size of golf balls seen from a medium distance. She draws up beside the car and goes no farther.*]

ARCHIE: You going in town like that?

11

BABY DOLL: Like what?

ARCHIE: In that there outfit. For a woman of your modest nature that squawks like a hen if her *husband* dast to put his hand on her, you sure do seem to be advertising your—

BABY DOLL [*drowning him out*]: My figure has filt out a little since I bought my trousseau AND paid for it with m'daddy's insurance money. I got two choices, wear clo'se skintight or go naked, now which do you want me t'—

ARCHIE: *Aw, now, hell! Will you git into th' car?*

[*Their angry voices are echoed by the wandering poultry.*]

BABY DOLL: I will git into the rear seat of that skatterbolt when you git out of the front seat and walk around here to open the door for me like a gentleman.

ARCHIE: Well, you gonna wait a long time if that's what you're waiting for!

BABY DOLL: I vow my father would turn over in his grave. . . .

ARCHIE: I never once did see your father get out and open a car door for your mother or any other woman. . . . Now get on in. . . .

[*She wheels about and her wedgies clack-clack down the drive. At foot of drive she assumes a hitchhiker's stance. A hot-rod skids to a sudden and noisy stop. Archie Lee bounds from his car like a jack rabbit, snatching a fistful of gravel as he plummets down drive. Hurls gravel at grinning teen-age kids in hot-rod, shouting incoherently as they shoot off, plunging Baby Doll and her protector in a dust-cloud. Through the dust . . .*]

12

ARCHIE: Got your license number you pack a—
DISSOLVE.

16A] THE CAR INTERIOR.
They are jolting down the road.

ARCHIE: Baby Doll, y'know they's no torture on earth to equal the torture which a cold woman inflicts on a man that she won't let touch her??!! No torture to compare with it! What I've done is!! Staked out a lot in hell, a lot with a rotten house on it and five complete sets of furniture not paid for. . . .

BABY DOLL: What you done is bit off more'n you can chew.

ARCHIE: People know the situation between us. Yestiddy on Front Street a man yelled to me, "Hey Archie Lee, has y'wife outgrowed the crib yet??" And three or four others haw-hawed! Public! Humiliation!

[*Baby Doll in back seat, her beads and earrings ajingle like a circus pony's harness.*]

BABY DOLL: Private humiliation is just as painful.

ARCHIE: Well! —There's an agreement between us! You ain't gonna sleep in no crib tomorrow night, Baby, when we celebrate your birthday.

BABY DOLL: If they remove those five complete sets of furniture from the house, I sure will sleep in the crib because the crib's paid for—I'll sleep in the crib or on the top of Aunt Rose Comfort's pianner. . . .

ARCHIE: And I want to talk to you about Aunt Rose Comfort. . . . I'm not in a position to feed and keep her any—

BABY DOLL: Look here, Big Shot, the day Aunt Rose Comfort is unwelcome under your roof . . .

ARCHIE: Baby Doll, honey, we just got to unload ourselves of all unnecessary burdens. . . . Now she can't cook and she—

BABY DOLL: If you don't like Aunt Rose Comfort's cooking, then get me a regular servant. I'm certainly not going to cook for a fat ole thing like you, money wouldn't pay me— Owwwww!

[*Archie has backhanded her. And prepares to do so again.*]

BABY DOLL: Cut that out. . . .

ARCHIE: You better quit saying "fat ole thing" about me!!

BABY DOLL: Well, you get young and thin and I'll quit calling you a fat old thing. —What's the matter now?

[*Archie Lee points to off right with a heavily tragic gesture.*]

17] TRAVELING SHOT. SYNDICATE GIN. THEIR VIEWPOINT.
It is new, handsome, busy, clearly prospering. A sign (large) reads:
SYNDICATE COTTON GIN.

18] TWO SHOT. ARCHIE AND BABY DOLL.

ARCHIE: There it is! There it is!

BABY DOLL: Looks like they gonna have a celebration!

ARCHIE: Why shouldn't they!!?? They now got every last bit

of business in the county, including every last bit of what I used to get.

BABY DOLL: Well, no wonder, they got an up-to-date plant— not like that big pile of junk you got!!

[*Archie glares at her.*]

QUICK DISSOLVE.

19] WAITING ROOM. DOCTOR'S OFFICE.
Archie and Baby Doll enter, and he is still hotly pursuing the same topic of discussion.

ARCHIE: Now I'm just as fond of Aunt Rose Comfort—

BABY DOLL: You ain't just as fond of Aunt—

ARCHIE: Suppose she breaks down on us?? Suppose she gets a disease that lingers—

[*Baby Doll snorts.*]

ARCHIE: All right, but I'm serving you notice. If that ole woman breaks down and dies on my place, I'm not going to be stuck with her funeral expenses. I'll have her burned up, yep, cremated, cremated, is what they call it. And pack her ashes in an ole Coca-Cola bottle and pitch the bottle into TIGER TAIL BAYOU!!!

BABY DOLL [*crossing to inner door*]: Doctor John? Come out here and take a look at my husband. I think a mad dawg's bit him. He's gone ravin' crazy!!

RECEPTIONIST [*appearing*]: Mr. Meighan's a little bit late for his appointment, but the doctor will see him.

15

BABY DOLL: Good! I'm going down to the—

ARCHIE: Oh, no, you're gonna sit here and wait till I come out. . . .

BABY DOLL: Well, maybe. . . .

[*Archie observes that she is exchanging a long, hard stare with a young man slouched in a chair.*]

ARCHIE: And look at this! Or somethin'.

[*He thrusts a copy of* Screen Secrets *into her hands and shoves her into a chair. Then glares at the young man, who raises his copy of* Confidential.]

DISSOLVE.

20] INNER OFFICE.
Archie Lee has been stripped down to the waist. The doctor has just finished examining him. From the anteroom, laughter, low, which seems to make Archie Lee nervous.

DOCTOR: You're not an old man, Archie Lee, but you're not a young man, either.

ARCHIE: That's the truth.

DOCTOR: How long you been married?

ARCHIE: Just about a year now.

DOCTOR: Have you been under a strain? You seem terrible nervous?

ARCHIE: No strain at all! None at all. . . .

16

[*Sound of low laughter from the waiting room. Suddenly, Archie Lee rushes over and opens the door. Baby Doll and the Young Man are talking. He quickly raises his magazine. . . . Archie closes the door, finishes dressing. . . .*]

DOCTOR: What I think you need is a harmless sort of sedative. . . .

ARCHIE: Sedative! Sedative! What do I want with a sedative???

[*He bolts out of the office. . . .*]

DISSOLVE.

21] MEDIUM LONG SHOT. ARCHIE LEE'S CAR GOING DOWN FRONT STREET.
Baby Doll sits on her side aloof. Suddenly a moving van passes the other way. On its side is marked the legend: IDEAL PAY AS YOU GO PLAN FURNITURE COMPANY. Suddenly, Baby Doll jumps up and starts waving her hand, flagging the van down, then when this fails, flagging Archie Lee down.

22] CLOSER SHOT. ARCHIE'S CAR.

BABY DOLL: That was all our stuff!

ARCHIE: No it wasn't. . . .

BABY DOLL: That was our stuff. Turn around, go after them.

ARCHIE: Baby Doll, I've got to wait down here for my perscription. . . .

[*At this moment another IDEAL PAY AS YOU GO PLAN FURNITURE COMPANY goes by, in the OTHER direction.*]

17

BABY DOLL: There goes another one, towards our house.

ARCHIE: Baby, let's go catch the show at the Delta Brilliant.

[*Baby Doll starts beating him.*]

Or let's drive over to the Flaming Pig and have some barbecue ribs and a little cold beer.

BABY DOLL: That's our stuff . . . !

[*Archie Lee looks the other way.*]

I said that's our stuff . . . !! I wanta go home. HOME. NOW. If you don't drive me home now, I'll, I'll, I'll— Mr. Hanna. Mr. Gus Hanna. You live on Tiger Tail Road. . . .

ARCHIE: I'll drive you home.

[*He spins the car around and they start home.*]

23] EXTERIOR. MEIGHAN HOUSE. DAY.
Meighan's car turns in the drive. The van we saw is backed up to the house, and furniture is being removed from the house. Baby Doll runs among them and starts to beat the movers. They go right on with their work, paying no attention. After a time Aunt Rose puts her arms around Baby Doll and leads her into the house.

24] CLOSE SHOT. ARCHIE LEE.
He really is on a spot. Again he hears the sound of the Syndicate Cotton Gin. He makes the same sound, imitating it, he made earlier. He looks in its direction and spits. Then he gets out of the car and walks towards his empty home.

25] INTERIOR. MEIGHAN HOUSE. THE PARLOR.
Baby Doll is sobbing by the window. The screen door creaks to admit the hulking figure of Archie Lee.

ARCHIE [*approaching*]: Baby Doll . . .

BABY DOLL: Leave me alone in here. I don't want to sit in the same room with a man that would make me live in a house with no furniture.

ARCHIE: Honey, the old furniture we got left just needs to be spread out a little. . . .

BABY DOLL: My daddy would turn in his grave if he knew, he'd turn in his grave.

ARCHIE: Baby Doll, if your daddy turned in his grave as often as you say he'd turn in his grave, that old man would plow up the graveyard.

[*Somewhere outside Aunt Rose is heard singing: "Rock of Ages."*]

ARCHIE: She's out there pickin' roses in the yard just as if nothing at all had happened here. . . .

BABY DOLL: I'm going to move to the Kotton King Hotel. I'm going to move to the Kotton King Hotel. . . .

ARCHIE: No, you ain't, Baby Doll.

BABY DOLL: And I'm going to get me a job. The manager of the Kotton King Hotel carried my daddy's coffin, he'll give me work.

ARCHIE: What sort of work do you think you could do, Baby Doll?

BABY DOLL: I could curl hair in a beauty parlor or polish nails in a barbershop, I reckon, or I could be a hostess and smile at customers coming into a place.

ARCHIE: What place?

BABY DOLL: Any place! I could be a cashier.

. ARCHIE: You can't count change.

BABY DOLL: I could pass out menus or programs or something and say hello to people coming in! [*Rises.*] I'll phone now.

[*She exits.*]

26] HALL.
Baby Doll crosses to the telephone. She is making herself attractive as if preparing for an interview.

BABY DOLL: Kotton King? This is Mrs. Meighan, I want to reserve a room for tomorrow mornin' and I want to register under my maiden name, which is Baby Doll McCorkle. My daddy was T.C. McCorkle who died last summer when I got married and he is a very close personal friend of the manager of the Kotton King Hotel—you know—what's his name. . . .

27] EXTERIOR OF HOUSE.
Archie comes out the door and wanders into the yard, passing Aunt Rose, who holds a bunch of roses.

AUNT ROSE: Archie Lee, look at these roses! Aren't they poems of nature?

ARCHIE: Uh-huh, poems of nature.

[*He goes past her, through the front gate and over to his Chevy.*

[*The front seat on the driver's side has been removed and a broken-down commodious armchair put in its place.*

20

[*Sound of the Syndicate Gin, throbbing. Archie Lee reaches under
the chair and fishes out a pint bottle. He takes a slug, listens to the
Syndicate, takes another. Then he throws the bottle out of the car,
turns the ignition key of the car and. . . .*]

28] THE CHEVY ROCKS OUT OF THE YARD. DIS-
SOLVE.

29] THE INTERIOR. BRITE SPOT CAFE.
*A habitually crowded place. Tonight it is empty. In the corner a
customer or two. Behind the bar, the man in the white apron with
nothing to do is sharpening a frog gig on a stone. Enter Archie, goes
over to the bar.*

ARCHIE: Didn't get to the bank today, Billy, so I'm a little
short of change. . . .

[*The Bartender has heard this before. He reaches to a low shelf and
takes out an unlabeled bottle and pours Archie a jolt.*]

ARCHIE: Thanks. Where's everybody?

BARTENDER: Over to the Syndicate Gin. Free liquor over
there tonight. Why don't you go over?

[*Then he laughs sardonically.*]

ARCHIE: What's the occasion?

BARTENDER: First anniversary. Why don't you go over and
help them celebrate.

ARCHIE: I'm not going to my own funeral either.

BARTENDER: I might as well lock up and go home. All that's
coming in here is such as you.

21

ARCHIE: What you got there?

[*The Bartender holds up a frog gig. The ends, where just sharpened, glisten.*]

ARCHIE: Been getting any frogs lately?

BARTENDER: Every time I go out. Going tomorrow night and get me a mess. You wanna come? There's a gang going. You look like you could use some fresh meat.

[*Another rather despondent-looking character comes in.*]

ARCHIE: Hey, Mac, how you doing?

MAC: Draggin', man.

BARTENDER: Why ain't you over to the Syndicate like everybody else?

MAC: What the hell would I do over that place. . . . That place ruined me . . . ruined me. . . .

BARTENDER: The liquor's running free over there tonight. And they got fireworks and everything. . . .

MAC: Fireworks! I'd like to see the whole place up in smoke. [*Confidentially.*] Say, I'm good for a couple, ain't I?

[*As the Bartender reaches for the same bottle-without-a-label, we*]
DISSOLVE TO:

30] EXTERIOR. SYNDICATE GIN.
A big platform has been built for the celebration and decked out with flags, including the Stars and Bars of Dixie and the Mississippi State Banner.

A band is playing "Mississippi Millions Love You," the state song, which is being sung by an emotional spinster. Several public officials are present, not all of them happy to be there as the county has a strongly divided attitude towards the Syndicate-owned plantation. Some old local ward heeler is reeling onto the speaker's platform and a signal is given to stop the band music. The Old Boy lifts a tin cup, takes a long swallow and remarks.

THE OLD BOY: Strongest branch water that ever wet my whistle. Must of come out of Tiger Tail Bayou.

[There is a great haw-haw.]

THE OLD BOY [*continuing*]: Young man? Mr. Vacarro. This is a mighty fine party you're throwing tonight to celebrate your first anniversary as superintendent of the Syndicate Plantation and Gin. And I want you to know that all of us good neighbors are proud of your achievement, bringin' in the biggest cotton crop ever picked off the blessed soil of Two River County.

[The camera has picked up a handsome, cocky young Italian, Silva Vacarro. His affability is not put on, but he has a way of darting glances right and left as he chuckles and drinks beer which indicates a certain watchfulness, a certain reserve.

[The camera has also picked up, among the other listeners, some uninvited guests . . . including Archie Lee and his friend from the Brite Spot. Archie Lee is well on the way and, of course, his resentment and bitterness are much more obvious.]

THE OLD BOY: Now when you first come here, well, we didn't know you yet and some of us old-timers were a little standoffish, at first.

[Vacarro's face has suddenly gone dark and sober. In his watchfulness he has noticed the hostile guests. With a sharp gesture of his

head, he summons a man who works for him—Rock—who comes up and kneels alongside. The following colloquy takes place right through The Old Boy's lines.]

SILVA: There's a handful of guys over there that don't look too happy to me. . . .

ROCK: They got no reason to be. You put 'em out of business when you built your own gin, and started to gin your own cotton.

SILVA: Watch 'em, keep an eye on 'em, specially if they start to wander around. . . .

THE OLD BOY [*who has continued*]: Natchully, a thing that is profitable to some is unprofitable to others. We all know that some people in this county have suffered some financial losses due in some measure to the success of the Syndicate Plantation.

[*Vacarro is looking around again, rather defiantly, but at no one in particular. Between the knees of his corduroy riding breeches is a whip that he carries habitually, a braided leather riding crop.*]

THE OLD BOY: But as a whole, the community has reaped a very rich profit.

[*He has said this rather defiantly as if he knew he was bucking a certain tide. . . . A voice from the crowd.*]

VOICE: Next time you run for office you better run on the Republican ticket. Git the nigger vote, Fatso!

THE OLD BOY [*answering*]: Just look at the new construction been going on! Contractors, carpenters, lumbermen, not to mention the owner and proprietor of the Brite Spot down the road there! And not to mention—

24

[*Suddenly somebody throws something at the speaker, something liquid and sticky. Instantly, Rock and Vacarro spring up.* . . .]

ROCK: Who done that?!?!

SILVA [*crossing to front of platform*]: If anybody's got anything more to throw, well, here's your target, here's your standing target! The wop! the foreign wop!!

[*Big rhubarb. The Old Boy is wiping his face with a wad of paper napkins.*

[*Suddenly, we see that something in the middle distance is on fire. The wide dark fields begin to light up.*

[*Voices cry alarm. Shouts, cries. Everyone and everything is lit by the shaking radiance of the fire.*

[*Vacarro races towards the fire. It is in the gin building. The volatile dust explodes. Loaded wagons are being pushed away, by Negro field hands driven by Vacarro.*

[*A fire engine arrives. But it seems lax in its efforts and inefficient. A hose is pulled out, but there is insufficient water to play water on the blaze, and the hose itself falls short. The firemen are not merely ineffectual. Some seem actually indifferent. In fact, some of their faces express an odd pleasure in the flames, which they seem more interested in watching than fighting.*

[*Vacarro rushes among them exhorting, commanding, constantly gesturing with his short riding crop. In his frenzy, he lashes the crop at the man holding the fire hose. The man, resentfully, throws the end of the hose at Vacarro, who seizes the nozzle and walks directly towards and into the flames.*

[*Now men try to stop him. Vacarro turns the hose on them, driving them back and then goes into the flames. He disappears from sight. All we hear is his shouts in a foreign tongue.*

25

[*A wall collapses.*

[*The hose suddenly leaps about as if it has been freed. The crowd. Horrified. Then they see something. . . .*

[*Vacarro comes out. He holds aloft a small, gallon-size kerosene can. He strikes at his trouser bottoms, which are hot. He is on the point of collapse. Men rush to him and drag him to a safe distance. He clutches the can.*

[*They lay him out, and crouch around him. He is smudged and singed. He eyes open, look around.*

[*His viewpoint. From this distorted angle, lit by the victorious flames are a circle of faces which are either indifferent or downright unfriendly. Some cannot control a faint smile.*

[*Vacarro clutches the can, closes his eyes.*

[*Another wall collapses.*]

DISSOLVE.

31] EXTERIOR. MEIGHAN HOUSE. NIGHT.
Archie Lee's car turns into the drive. He descends noiselessly as a thief. Camera follows him, and it and he discover Baby Doll on the porch swing. There are several suitcases, packed and ready to go. In a chair near the porch swing, sleeping as mildly as a baby, is Aunt Rose Comfort.

ARCHIE: What are you doin' out here at one o'clock in the morning?

BABY DOLL: I'm not talking to you.

ARCHIE: What are you doing out here?

BABY DOLL: Because in the first place, I didn't have the money to pay for a hotel room, because you don't give me any money, because you don't have any money, and secondly, because if I had the money I couldn't have no way of getting there because you went off in the Chevy, and leave me no way of getting anywhere, including to the fire which I wanted to see just like everyone else.

ARCHIE: What fire you talking about?

BABY DOLL: What fire am I talking about?

ARCHIE: I don't know about no fire.

BABY DOLL: You must be crazy or think I'm crazy. You mean to tell me you don't know the cotton gin burned down at the Syndicate Plantation right after you left the house.

ARCHIE [*seizing her arm*]: Hush up. I never left this house.

BABY DOLL: You certainly did leave this house. OW!!

ARCHIE: Look here! Listen to what I tell you. I never left this house. . . .

BABY DOLL: You certainly did and left me here without a coke in the place. OWW!! Cut it out!!

ARCHIE: Listen to what I tell you. I went up to bed with my bottle after supper—

BABY DOLL: What bed! OW!

ARCHIE: And passed out dead to the world. You got that in your haid?? Will you remember that now?

27

BABY DOLL: Le' go my arm!

ARCHIE: What did I do after supper?

BABY DOLL: You know what you did, you jumped in the Chevy an' disappeared after supper and didn't get back till just — OWWW!!! Will you quit twisting my arm.

ARCHIE: I'm trying to wake you up. You're asleep, you're dreaming! What did I do after supper?

BABY DOLL: Went to bed! Leggo! Went to bed. Leggo! Leggo!

ARCHIE: That's right. Make sure you remember. I went to bed after supper and didn't wake up until I heard the fire whistle blow and I was too drunk to git up and drive the car. Now come inside and go to bed.

BABY DOLL: Go to what bed? I got no bed to go to!

ARCHIE: You will tomorrow. The furniture is coming back tomorrow.

[*Baby Doll whimpers.*]

ARCHIE [*continuing*]: Did I hurt my little baby's arm?

BABY DOLL: Yais.

ARCHIE: Where I hurt little baby's arm?

BABY DOLL: Here. . . .

ARCHIE [*putting a big wet kiss on her arm*]: Feel better?

BABY DOLL: No. . . .

ARCHIE [*another kiss, this travels up her arm*]: My sweet baby doll. My sweet little baby doll.

BABY DOLL [*sleepily*]: Hurt. . . . MMMmmmmm! Hurt.

ARCHIE: Hurt?

BABY DOLL: Mmm!

ARCHIE: Kiss?

BABY DOLL: Mmmmmmmmm.

ARCHIE: Baby sleepy?

BABY DOLL: MMmmmmm.

ARCHIE: Kiss good . . . ?

BABY DOLL: Mmmmm. . . .

ARCHIE: Make little room . . . good. . . .

BABY DOLL: Too hot.

ARCHIE: Make a little room, go on. . . .

BABY DOLL: Mmmm. . . .

ARCHIE: Whose baby? Big sweet . . . whose baby?

BABY DOLL: You hurt me. . . . Mmmm. . . .

ARCHIE: Kiss. . . .

[*He lifts her wrist to his lips and makes a gobbling sound. We get an idea of what their courtship—such as it was—was like. Also how passionately he craves her, willing to take her under any conditions, including fast asleep.*]

BABY DOLL: Stop it. . . . Silly. . . . Mmmmmm. . . .

ARCHIE: What would I do if you was a big piece of cake?

BABY DOLL: Silly.

ARCHIE: Gobble! Gobble!

BABY DOLL: Oh you. . . .

ARCHIE: What would I do if you was angel food cake? Big white piece with lots of nice thick icin'?

BABY DOLL [*giggling now, in spite of herself, also sleepy*]: Quit.

ARCHIE [*as close as he's ever been to having her*]: Gobble! Gobble! Gobble!

BABY DOLL: Archie!

ARCHIE: Hmmmmm. . . .

[*He's working on her arm.*]

Skrunch, gobble, ghrumpt . . . etc.

BABY DOLL: You tickle. . . .

ARCHIE: Answer little question. . . .

BABY DOLL: What?

ARCHIE [*into her arm*]: Where I been since supper?

BABY DOLL: Off in the Chevy—

[*Instantly he seizes her wrist again. She shrieks. The romance is over.*]

ARCHIE: Where I been since supper?

BABY DOLL: Upstairs. . . .

ARCHIE: Doing what?

BABY DOLL: With your bottle. Archie, leggo. . . .

ARCHIE: And what else. . . .

BABY DOLL: Asleep. Leggo. . . .

ARCHIE [*letting go*]: Now you know where I been and what I been doing since supper. In case anybody asks.

BABY DOLL: Yeah.

ARCHIE: Now go to sleep. . . .

[*He seizes her suitcases and goes off into the house. Baby Doll follows, and Aunt Rose follows her, asleep on her feet. As they go in, Archie Lee comes out and looks around. Then he listens.*]

ARCHIE: Nice quiet night. Real nice and quiet.

[*The gin can no longer be heard.*]

CUT TO:

32] BRITE SPOT CAFE. EXTERIOR. NIGHT.

It's not quiet here at all. The area in front of the entrance is crowded with cars. A holiday mood prevails. It's as if the fire has satisfied some profound and basic hunger and left the people of that community exhilarated.

The pickup truck of Silva Vacarro drives up, shoots into a vacant spot. He leaps from the driver's cab. He has not yet washed, his shirt is torn and blackened and he has a crude bandage around the arm that holds the whip. He stands for a few moments beside his truck, looking around at the cars, trying to find the car of the Marshal, which would indicate that that county official is inside. Then he sees what he's looking for. He walks over to the car which has the official seal on its side, and not finding the Marshal there, turns and strides into the . . .

33] INTERIOR. BRITE SPOT. (A JUKE JOINT.)
Everybody is talking about the fire. The juke box is a loud one. There are some dancing couples.

Silva Vacarro passes by a little knot of men. He is followed by Rock, holding the kerosene can. The camera stays with them. They smile.

A MAN: That ole boy is really burning!

[*One of the men detaches himself and moves in the direction that Vacarro took. Then another follows.*]

34] GROUP OF MEN AROUND THE MARSHAL.

MARSHAL: What makes you think your gin was set fire to?

SILVA: Look around you. Did you ever see such a crowd of happy faces, looks like a rich man's funeral with all his relations attending.

32

MARSHAL: I'd hate to have to prove it.

SILVA: I'd hate to have to depend on you to prove it.

[*The man from the other group walks up.*]

MAN: What are you going to do about ginning out your cotton?

SILVA: I'll truck it over to Sunset. Collins'll gin it out for me.

MAN: Collins got cotton of his own to gin.

SILVA: Then I'll truck it across the river. Ain't nobody around here's gonna gin it.

MAN: I'm all set up to do it for you.

SILVA: I wouldn't give you the satisfaction.

[*The men drift back a few steps.*]

MARSHAL [*speaking a little for the benefit of the men in the room*]: I honestly can't imagine if it was a case of arson who could of done it since every man jack that you put out of business was standing right there next to the platform when the fire broke out.

ROCK: One wasn't. I know one that wasn't.

MARSHAL [*wheeling on bar stool to face him, sharply*]: Looky here, boy! Naming names is risky, just on suspicion.

ROCK: I didn't name his name. I just said I know it. And the initials are stamped on this here can.

MARSHAL [*quickly*]: Let's break it up, break it up, not the time or the place to make accusations, I'll take charge of this can. I'll examine it carefully to see if there's any basis for thinking it was used to start a fire with.

SILVA [*cutting in*]: I run through fire to git that can, and I mean to keep it. [*Then to Rock:*] Lock it up in the pickup truck.

[*Rock leaves. Unobtrusively some men follow him.*]

MARSHAL: Vacarro. Come over here. I want to have a word with you in one of these booths. . . .

35] ROCK.
He enters the men's room. As he approaches the urinal, the light is switched out and the door is thrown open at the same moment. Hoarse muffled shouts and sounds of struggle and a metallic clatter. Then the light goes on and Rock is lying on the filthy cement floor, dazed. Vacarro enters. He goes to Rock.

ROCK: They got the can, boss.

SILVA: Whose initials was on it? Huh? You said you seen some initials on the can.

ROCK: Naw. It just said—Sears and Roebuck.

[*The Marshal has come in and now reaches down and helps Rock to regain his feet. . . .*]

MARSHAL: Sears and Roebuck! That does it! Hahaha. Boy, git up and git some black coffee in yuh.

[*They pass through the door.*]

36] THE MAIN ROOM.

MARSHAL: Ruby, Ruby! Give this boy some black coffee. He had a bad fall in the outhouse. Hawhawhaw. . . .

[*But Silva has steered Rock out the front door and they are gone. The Marshal follows . . .*]

37] OUTSIDE.
Silva and Rock head towards the pickup. The Marshal appears in the doorway.

MARSHAL: Vacarro!

[*Silva and Rock are at the truck. They wait for the Marshal, who is walking towards them.*]

MARSHAL [*soberly, plainly*]: You take the advice of an old man who knows this county like the back of his hand. It's true you made a lot of enemies here. You happen to be a man with foreign blood. That's a disadvantage in this county. A disadvantage at least to begin with. But you added stubbornness and suspicion and resentment.

[*Vacarro makes an indescribable sound.*]

MARSHAL: I still say, a warm, friendly attitude on your part could have overcome that quickly. Instead, you stood off from people, refused to fraternize with them. Why not drop that attitude now? If some one set fire to your gin—I say that's not impossible. Also, I say we'll find him. But I don't have to tell you that if you now take your cotton across the river, or into another county, it will give rise to a lot of unfriendly speculation. No one would like it. No one.

[*Abruptly he turns and goes.*

[*Rock and Silva are left alone. Men watch them from the surrounding cars . . . from the doorway.*]

SILVA: Did you ever see so many happy faces? Which one did it, Rock, you said you knew . . . ?

ROCK: Well, they're all here . . . all here except one. The one that ain't here, I figure he did it. . . .

[*They're getting into the pickup.*]

SILVA: Well, he's the one that's gonna gin out my cotton. . . .

[*The motor starts . . . the car goes into gear . . . and moves.*]
DISSOLVE.

38] THE ROAD BEFORE THE MEIGHAN HOUSE.
THE NEXT MORNING.
Silva's pickup truck is leading a long line of cotton wagons—full of cotton.

39] CLOSER SHOT. THE PICKUP.
It stops.

40] CLOSE ANGLE. SILVA AND ROCK.

ROCK: Maybe it figures. But it sure puzzles me why you want to bring your cotton to the guy that burned down your gin. . . .

SILVA: You don't know the Christian proverb about how you turn the other cheek when one has been slapped. . . .

ROCK: When both cheeks has been kicked, what are you gonna turn then?

SILVA: You just got to turn and keep turning. Stop the wagons! I'm gonna drive up to his house.

[*Rock hops out of the pickup truck.*]

41] OUTSIDE MEIGHAN HOUSE.

At an upstairs window we can just see Archie's face. He is watching the wagons. Suddenly, he withdraws his head.

42] UPSTAIRS. MEIGHAN HOUSE.

He goes into a crazy, but silent Indian war dance. Then suddenly he can no longer contain himself and runs into . . .

43] THE NURSERY.

Enter Archie Lee.

Baby Doll is asleep in the crib. Her thumb is in her mouth. Like a child, she's trying to hold on to her sleep. Archie Lee just whoops and hollers. "Baby Doll! Baby Doll!", etc. "Get up . . ." etc.

She can hardly believe her eyes. . . .

From downstairs the pickup's horn sounds urgently.

Aunt Rose Comfort rushes in breathlessly . . .

AUNT ROSE: Archie Lee, honesy. . . .

ARCHIE [*very big shot*]: Get her up! Get her up, get her washed and dressed and looking decent. Then bring her down. The furniture is coming back today. . . .

[*He exits.* . . .]

44]–65] FRONT YARD.

Silva and Rock are sitting there in the pickup truck. They sit a little formally and stiffly and wait for Meighan, who comes barreling out of the house, and up to the pickup.

ARCHIE: Don't say a word. A little bird already told me that you'd be bringing those twenty-seven wagons full of cotton straight to my door, and I want you to know that you're a very lucky fellow.

ROCK [*dryly*]: How come?

ARCHIE: I mean that I am in a position to hold back other orders and give you a priority. Well! Come on out of that truck and have some coffee.

SILVA: What's your price?

ARCHIE: You remember my price. It hasn't changed.

[*Silence. The sense that Silva is inspecting him.*]

ARCHIE: Hey, now looka here. Like you take shirts to a laundry. You take them Friday and you want them Saturday. That's special. You got to pay special.

SILVA: How about your equipment? Hasn't changed either?

ARCHIE: A-1 shape! Always was! You ought to remember.

SILVA: I remember you needed a new saw-cylinder. You got one?

ARCHIE: Can't find one on the market to equal the old one yet. Come on down and have a cup of coffee. We're all ready for you.

SILVA: I guess when you saw my gin burning down last night you must've suspected that you might get a good deal of business thrown your way in the morning.

ARCHIE: You want to know something?

SILVA: I'm always glad to know something when there's something to know.

[*Rock laughs wildly.*]

ARCHIE: I never seen that fire of yours last night! Now come on over to my house and have some coffee.

[*The men get out of the truck. Archie speaks to Rock.*]

ARCHIE: You come too, if you want to. . . . No, sir, I never seen that fire of yours last night. We hit the sack right after supper and didn't know until breakfast time this morning that your cotton gin had burned down.

[*They go up on the porch.*]

Yes sir, it's providential. That's the only word for it. Hey, Baby Doll! It's downright providential. Baby Doll! Come out here, Baby Doll!

[*Enter Baby Doll.*]

You come right over here and meet Mr. Vacarro from the Syndicate Plantation.

BABY DOLL: Oh hello. Has something gone wrong, Archie Lee?

ARCHIE: What do you mean, Baby Doll?

BABY DOLL: I just thought that maybe something went—

ARCHIE: What is your first name, Vacarro?

SILVA: Silva.

ARCHIE: How do you spell it?

[*Silva spells it. "Capital S-I-L-V-A." Meantime, his eyes are on Baby Doll.*]

ARCHIE: Oh. Like a silver lining? Every cloud has got a silver lining.

BABY DOLL: What is that from? The Bible?

SILVA: No, the Mother Goose book.

BABY DOLL: That name sounds foreign.

SILVA: It is, Mrs. Meighan. I'm known as the wop that runs the Syndicate Plantation.

[*Archie Lee claps him heartily on the back. Silva stiffly withdraws from the contact.*]

ARCHIE: Don't call yourself names. Let other folks call you names! Well, you're a lucky little fellow, silver, gold, or even nickel-plated, you sure are lucky that I can take a job of this size right now. It means some cancellations, but you're my closest neighbor. I believe in the good neighbor policy, Mr. Vacarro. You do me a good turn and I'll do you a good turn. Tit for tat. Tat for tit is the policy we live on. *Aunt Rose Comfort!* Baby Doll, git your daddy's ole maid sister to break out a fresh pot of coffee for Mr. Vacarro.

BABY DOLL: You get her.

ARCHIE: And honey, I want you to entertain this gentleman. Ha! Ha! Look at her blush. Haha! This is my baby. This is my little girl, every precious ounce of her is mine, all mine.

40

[*He exits—crazily elated, calling "Aunt Rose."*

[CUT BACK *to Baby Doll. She emits an enormous yawn.*]

BABY DOLL: Excuse my yawn. We went to bed kinda late last night.

[CUT TO SILVA. *He notices the discrepancy. He looks at Rock, who also noticed.*

[*As if she were talking of a title of great distinction.*]

So. You're a wop?

SILVA [*with ironic politeness*]: I'm a Sicilian, Mrs. Meighan. A very ancient people. . . .

BABY DOLL [*trying out the word*]: Sish! Sish!

SILVA: No Ma'am. Siss! Sicilian.

BABY DOLL: Oh, how unusual.

[*Archie Lee bursts back out on the porch.*]

ARCHIE: And honey, at noon, take Mr. Vacarro in town to the Kotton King Hotel for a chicken dinner. Sign my name! It's only when bad luck hits you, Mr. Vacarro, that you find out who your friends are. I mean to prove it. All right. Let's get GOING! Baby, knock me a kiss!

BABY DOLL: What's the matter with you? Have you got drunk before breakfast?

ARCHIE: Hahaha.

BABY DOLL: Somebody say something funny?

ARCHIE: Offer this young fellow here to a cup of coffee. I got to get busy ginning that cotton.

[*He extends his great sweaty hand to Vacarro.*]

Glad to be able to help you out of this bad situation. It's the good neighbor policy.

SILVA: What is?

ARCHIE: You do me a good turn and I'll do you a good turn sometime in the future.

SILVA: I see.

ARCHIE: Tit for tat, tat for tit, as they say. Hahaha! Well, make yourself at home here. Baby Doll, I want you to make this gentleman comfortable in the house.

BABY DOLL: You can't make anyone comfortable in this house. Lucky if you can find a chair to sit in.

[*But Meighan is gone, calling out: "Move those wagons," etc., etc.*]

BABY DOLL [*after a slight pause*]: Want some coffee?

SILVA: No. Just a cool drink of water, thank you ma'am.

BABY DOLL: The kitchen water runs warm, but if you got the energy to handle an old-fashioned pump, you can get you a real cool drink from that there cistern at the side of the house. . . .

SILVA: I got energy to burn.

[*Vacarro strides through the tall seeding grass to an old cistern with a hand pump, deep in the side yard. Rock follows. Old Fussy goes "Squawk, Squawk," and Aunt Rose Comfort is singing "Rock of Ages" in the kitchen.*]

SILVA [*looking about contemptuously as he crosses to the cistern*]: Dump their garbage in the yard, phew! *Ignorance* and *indulgence* and *stink!*

ROCK: I thought that young Mizz Meighan smelt pretty good.

SILVA: You keep your nose with the cotton. And hold that dipper, I'll pump.

AUNT ROSE: Sometimes water comes and sometimes it don't.

[*The water comes pouring from the rusty spout.*]

SILVA: This time it did. . . .

BABY DOLL: Bring me a dipper of that nice cool well water, please.

[*Rock crosses immediately with the filled dipper.*]

SILVA: Hey!

OLD FUSSY: Squawk, squawk!!

AUNT ROSE: I don't have the strength anymore in my arm that I used to, to draw water out of that pump.

[*She approaches, smoothing her ancient apron. Vacarro is touched by her aged grace.*]

SILVA: Would you care for a drink?

43

AUNT ROSE: How do you do? I'm Aunt Rose Comfort McCorkle. My brother was Baby Doll's daddy, Mr. T. C. McCorkle. I've been visiting here since . . . since. . . .

[*She knits her ancient brow, unable to recall precisely when the long visit started.*]

SILVA: I hope you don't mind drinking out of a gourd.

[*He hands her the gourd of well water. Rock returns, saying aloud . . .*]

ROCK: I could think of worse ways to spend a hot afternoon than delivering cool well water to Mrs. Meighan.

AUNT ROSE: SCUSE ME PLEASE! That ole hen, Fussy, has just gone back in my kitchen!

[*She runs crazily to the house. Baby Doll has wandered back to the cistern as if unconsciously drawn by the magnetism of the two young males.*]

BABY DOLL: They's such a difference in water! You wouldn't think so, but there certainly is.

SILVA [*to Rock*]: Hold the dipper, I'll pump!

[*He brings up more water; then strips off his shirt and empties the brimming dipper over his head and at the same time he says to Rock . . .*]

SILVA: Go stay with the cotton. Go on! Stay with the cotton.

[*Rock goes.*]

BABY DOLL: I wouldn't dare to expose myself like that. I take such terrible sunburn.

44

SILVA: I like the feel of a hot sun on my body.

BABY DOLL: That's not sunburn though. You're natcherally dark.

SILVA: Yes. Don't you have garbage collectors on Tiger Tail Road?

BABY DOLL: It cost a little bit extra to get them to come out here and Archie Lee Meighan claimed it was highway robbery! Refused to pay! Now the place is swarming with flies an' mosquitoes and—oh, I don't know, I almost give up sometimes.

SILVA: And did I understand you to say that you've got a bunch of unfurnished rooms in the house?

BABY DOLL: Five complete sets of furniture hauled away! By the Ideal Pay As You Go Plan Furniture Company.

SILVA: When did this misfortune—fall upon you?

BABY DOLL: Why yestiddy! Ain't that awful?

SILVA: Both of us had misfortunes on the same day.

BABY DOLL: Huh?

SILVA: You lost your furniture. My cotton gin burned down.

BABY DOLL [*not quite with it*]: Oh.

SILVA: Quite a coincidence!

BABY DOLL: Huh?

SILVA: I said it was a coincidence of misfortune.

BABY DOLL: Well, sure—after all what can you do with a bunch of unfurnished rooms.

SILVA: Well, you could play hide-and-seek.

BABY DOLL: Not me. I'm not athletic.

SILVA: I take it you've not had this place long, Mrs. Meighan.

BABY DOLL: No, we ain't had it long.

SILVA: When I arrived in this county to take over the management of the Syndicate Plantation . . .

[*He chops at the grass with his crop.*]

this place was empty. I was told it was haunted. Then you all moved in.

BABY DOLL: Yes it was haunted, and that's why Archie Lee bought it for almost nothing.

[*She pauses in the sun as if dazed.*]

Sometimes I don't know where to go, what to do.

SILVA: That's not uncommon. People enter this world without instruction.

BABY DOLL [*she's lost him again*]: Huh?

SILVA: I said people come into this world without instructions of where to go, what to do, so they wander a little and . . .

[*Aunt Rose sings rather sweetly from the kitchen, wind blows an Aeolian refrain.*]

46

then go away. . . .

[*Now Baby Doll gives him a quick look, almost perceptive and then . . .*]

BABY DOLL: Yah, well . . .

SILVA: *Drift*—for a while and then . . . *vanish.*

[*He stoops to pick a dandelion.*]

And so make room for newcomers! Old goers, new comers! Back and forth, going and coming, rush, rush!! *Permanent? Nothing!*

[*Blows on the seeding dandelion.*]

Anything living! . . . last long enough to take it serious.

[*They are walking together. There is the beginning of some weird understanding between them.*

[*They have stopped strolling by a poetic wheelless chassis of an old Pierce Arrow limousine in the side yard.*]

BABY DOLL: This is the old Pierce Arrow car that belonged to the lady that used to own this place and haunts it now.

[*Vacarro steps gravely forward and opens the back door for her.*]

SILVA: Where to, madam?

BABY DOLL: Oh, you're playing *show-fer!* It's a good place to sit when the house isn't furnished. . . .

[*She enters and sinks on the ruptured upholstery. He gravely puts the remnant of the dandelion in the cone-shaped cut-glass vase in a bracket by the back seat of the old limousine.*]

47

BABY DOLL [*laughing with sudden, childish laughter*]: Drive me along the river as fast as you can with all the windows open to cool me off.

SILVA: Fine, Madam!

BABY DOLL [*suddenly aware of his body near her*]: Showfers sit in the front seat.

SILVA: Front seat's got no cushion.

BABY DOLL: It's hard to find a place to sit around here since the Ideal Pay As You Go Plan people lost patience. To sit in comfort, I mean. . . .

SILVA: It's hard to sit in comfort when the Ideal Pay As You Go Plan people lose their patience and your gin burns down.

BABY DOLL: Oh! But . . .

SILVA: Huh?

BABY DOLL: You said that like you thought there was . . .

SILVA: What?

BABY DOLL: Some connection! Excuse me, I want to get out and I can't get over your legs. . . .

[*Her apathy is visited by a sudden inexplicable flurry of panic. He has his boots propped against the back of the front seat.*]

SILVA: You can't get over my legs?

BABY DOLL: No. I'm not athletic.

[*She tries to open the door on the other side, but it is blocked by the trunk of a pecan tree.*]

SILVA: But it's cool here and comfortable to sit in. What's this here??

[*He has seized her wrist on which hangs a bracelet of many little gold charms. She sinks somewhat uneasily in beside him.*]

BABY DOLL: It's a, it's a . . . charm bracelet.

[*He begins to finger the many little gold charms attached.*]

BABY DOLL: My daddy gave it to me. Them there's the ten commandments.

SILVA: And these?

BABY DOLL: My birthdays. It's stretchable. One for each birthday.

SILVA: How many charming birthdays have you had?

BABY DOLL: As many as I got charms hanging on that bracelet.

SILVA: Mind if I count 'em?

[*They are close.*]

. . . fourteen, fifteen, sixteen, seventeen, eighteen, nineteen, and . . .

BABY DOLL: That's all. I'll be twenty tomorrow. Tomorrow is Election Day and Election Day is my birthday. I was born on the day that Frank Delano Roosevelt was elected for his first term.

SILVA: A great day for the country for both reasons.

BABY DOLL: He was a man to respect.

SILVA: And you're a lady to respect, Mrs. Meighan.

BABY DOLL [*sadly and rather touchingly*]: Me? Oh, no—I never got past the fourth grade.

SILVA: Why'd you quit?

BABY DOLL: I had a great deal of trouble with long division. . . .

SILVA: Yeah?

BABY DOLL: The teacher would tell me to go to the blackboard and work out a problem in long division and I would go to the blackboard and lean my head against it and cry and cry and—cry. . . .

Whew! I think the porch would be cooler. Mr. Vacarro, I can't get over your legs.

SILVA: You want to move my legs.

BABY DOLL: Yes, otherwise, I can't get out of the car. . . .

SILVA: Okay.

[*He raises his legs so she can get out. Which she does, and continues . . .*]

BABY DOLL: YES, I would cry and cry. . . . Well . . . soon after that I left school. A girl without education is—without education. . . .

Whew. . . . Feel kind of dizzy. Hope I'm not gettin' a *sun* stroke. —I better sit in the shade. . . .

[*Vacarro follows her casually into the shade of the pecan tree where there's a decrepit old swing. Suddenly, he leaps into the branches and then down with a pecan. He cracks it in his mouth and hands her the kernels. . . .*]

BABY DOLL: Mr. Vacarro! I wouldn't dream! —excuse me, but I just wouldn't dream! of eating a nut that a man had cracked in his mouth. . . .

SILVA: You've got many refinements. I don't think you need to worry about your failure at long division. I mean, after all, you got through short division, and short division is all that a lady ought to be called on to cope with. . . .

BABY DOLL: Well, I—ought to go in, but I get depressed when I pass through those empty rooms. . . .

SILVA: All the rooms empty?

BABY DOLL: All but the nursery. And the kitchen. The stuff in those rooms was paid for. . . .

SILVA: You have a child in the nursery?

BABY DOLL: Me? No. I sleep in the nursery myself. Let down the slats on the crib. . . .

SILVA: Why do you sleep in the nursery?

BABY DOLL: Mr. Vacarro, that's a *personal* question.

[*There is a pause.*]

51

BABY DOLL: I ought to go in . . . but . . . you know there are places in that house which I never been in. I mean the attic for instance. Most of the time I'm afraid to go into that house by myself. Last night when the fire broke out I sat here on this swing for hours and hours till Archie Lee got home, because I was scared to enter this old place by myself.

[*Vacarro has caught this discrepancy too.*]

SILVA: It musta been scary here without your husband to look after you.

BABY DOLL: I'm tellin' you! The fire lit up the whole country-side and it made big crazy shadows and we didn't have a coke in the house and the heat and the mosquitoes and—I was mad at Archie Lee.

SILVA: Mad at Mr. Meighan? What about?

BABY DOLL: Oh, he went off and left me settin' here without a coke in the place.

SILVA: Went off and left you, did he??!!

BABY DOLL: Well, he certainly did. Right after supper and when he got back, the fire'd already broke out. I got smoke in my eyes and my nose and throat. I was in such a wornout nervous condition it made me cry. Finally I took two teaspoons of paregoric.

SILVA: Sounds like you passed a very uncomfortable night.

BABY DOLL: Sounds like? Well it was!

SILVA: So Mr. Meighan—you say—disappeared after supper.

52

BABY DOLL [*after a pause*]: Huh?

SILVA: You say Mr. Meighan left the house for a while after supper?

[*Something in his tone makes her aware that she has spoken indiscreetly.*]

BABY DOLL: Oh—uh—just for a moment.

SILVA: Just for a moment, huh? How long a moment?

BABY DOLL: What are you driving at, Mr. Vacarro?

SILVA: Driving at? Nothing.

BABY DOLL: You're looking at me so funny.

SILVA: How long a moment did he disappear for? Can you remember, Mrs. Meighan?

BABY DOLL: What difference does that make? What's it to you, anyhow?

SILVA: Why should you mind my asking?

BABY DOLL: You make this sound like I was on trial for something.

SILVA: Don't you like to pretend like you're a witness?

BABY DOLL: Witness of what, Mr. Vacarro?

SILVA: Why—for instance—say—a case of arson!

BABY DOLL: Case of—? What is—arson?

53

SILVA: The willful destruction of property by fire.

[*He slaps his boots sharply with the riding crop.*]

BABY DOLL: Oh!

[*She nervously fingers her purse.*]

SILVA: There's one thing I always notice about you ladies.

BABY DOLL: What's that?

SILVA: Whenever you get nervous, you always like to have something in your hands to hold on to—like that big white purse.

BABY DOLL: This purse?

SILVA: Yes, it gives you something to hold on to, isn't that right?

BABY DOLL: Well, I do always like to have something in my hands.

SILVA: Sure you do. You feel what a lot of uncertain things there are. Gins burn down. No one know how or why. Volunteer fire departments don't have decent equipment. They're no protection. The afternoon sun is too hot. The trees! They're no protection! The house—it's haunted! It's no protection. Your husband. He's across the road and busy. He's no protection! The goods that dress is made of—it's light and thin—it's no protection. So what do you do, Mrs. Meighan? You pick up that white kid purse. It's something to hold on to.

BABY DOLL: Now, Mr. Vacarro. Don't you go and be getting any—funny ideas.

SILVA: Ideas about what?

BABY DOLL: My husband disappearing—after supper. I can explain that.

SILVA: Can you?

BABY DOLL: Sure I can.

SILVA: Good! How do you explain it?

[*He stares at her. She looks down.*]

What's the matter? Can't you collect your thoughts, Mrs. Meighan?

[*Pause.*]

Your mind's a blank on the subject?

BABY DOLL: Look here, now. . . .

SILVA: You find it impossible to remember just what your husband disappeared for after supper? You can't imagine what kind of an errand he went out on, can you?

BABY DOLL: No! No! I can't!

SILVA: But when he returned—let's see—the fire had just broken out at the Syndicate Plantation.

BABY DOLL: Mr. Vacarro, I don't have the slightest idea what you could be driving at.

SILVA: You're a very unsatisfactory witness, Mrs. Meighan.

55

BABY DOLL: I never can think when people—stare straight at me.

SILVA: Okay, I'll look away then.

[*Turns his back to her.*]

Now, does that improve your memory any? Now are you able to concentrate on the question?

BABY DOLL: Huh?

SILVA: No? You're not?

[*Grins evilly.*]

Well—should we drop the subject??

BABY DOLL: I sure do wish you would!

SILVA: Sure, there's no use crying over a burnt-down gin. And besides, like your husband says—this world is built on the principle of tit for tat.

BABY DOLL: What do you mean?

SILVA: Nothing at all specific. Mind if I . . . ?

BABY DOLL: What?

[*Silva approaches the swing where she sits.*]

SILVA: You want to move over a little and make some room?

BABY DOLL [*shifting slightly*]: Is that room enough for you?

SILVA: Enough for me. How about you?

BABY DOLL: Is it strong enough to support us both?

SILVA: I hope. Let's swing a little. You seem all tense. Motion relaxes people. It's like a cradle. A cradle relaxes a baby. They call you "Baby," don't they?

BABY DOLL: That's sort of a pet name.

SILVA: Well in the swing you can relax like a cradle. . . .

BABY DOLL: Not if you swing it so high. It shakes me up.

SILVA: Well, I'll swing it low then. Are you relaxed?

BABY DOLL: I'm relaxed enough. As much as necessary.

SILVA: No, you're not. Your nerves are all tied up.

BABY DOLL: You make me nervous.

SILVA: Just swinging with you?

BABY DOLL: Not just that.

SILVA: What else then?

BABY DOLL: All them questions you asked me about the fire.

SILVA: I only inquired about your husband—about his leaving the house after supper.

BABY DOLL: Why should I have to explain why he left the house? Besides, I did. I think I explained that to you.

SILVA: You said that he left the house before the fire broke out.

57

BABY DOLL: What about it?

SILVA: Why did he leave the house?

BABY DOLL: I explained that to you. I explained that to you.

SILVA: What was the explanation? I forgot it.

[*Baby Doll's face is beaded with sweat. To save her life she can't think, can't think at all.*]

BABY DOLL [*just to gain a moment*]: Oh, you're talking about my husband?

SILVA: That's who I'm talking about.

BABY DOLL: How should I know!!!

SILVA: You mean where he went after supper.

BABY DOLL: Yes!! How should I know where he went.

SILVA: I thought you said you explained that to me.

BABY DOLL: I did! I explained it to you!

SILVA: Well, if you don't know, how could you explain it to me?

BABY DOLL [*turning*]: There's no reason why I should explain things to you.

SILVA: Then just relax.

[*They swing.*]

As I was saying, that was a lovely remark your husband made.

BABY DOLL: What remark did he make?

SILVA: The good neighbor policy. I see what he means by that now.

BABY DOLL: He was talking about the President's speech.

SILVA: I think he was talking about something closer to home. *You do me* a good turn and *I'll do you* one. That was the way he put it.

[*Delicately he removes a little piece of lint from her arm.*]

SILVA: There now!

BABY DOLL [*nervously*]: Thanks.

SILVA: There's a lot of fine cotton lint floating around in the air.

BABY DOLL: I know there is. It irritates my sinus.

SILVA: Well, you're a delicate woman.

BABY DOLL: Delicate? Me? Oh no. I'm a good-size woman.

SILVA: There's a lot of you, but every bit of you is delicate. Choice. Delectable, I might say.

BABY DOLL: Huh?

SILVA [*running his finger lightly over her skin*]: You're fine fibered. And smooth. And soft.

BABY DOLL: Our conversation is certainly taking a personal turn!

SILVA: Yes! You make me think of cotton.

[*Still caressing her arm another moment.*]

No! No fabric, no kind of cloth, not even satin or silk cloth, or no kind of fiber, not even cotton fiber has the ab-so-lute delicacy of your skin!

BABY DOLL: Well! Should I say thanks or something?

SILVA: No, just smile, Mrs. Meighan. You have an attractive smile. Dimples!!

BABY DOLL: No . . .

SILVA: Yes, you have! Smile, Mrs. Meighan! Come on! Smile!

[*Baby Doll averts her face, smiles helplessly.*]

There now. See? You've got them!

[*Delicately, he touches one of the indentations in her cheek.*]

BABY DOLL: Please don't touch me. I don't like to be touched.

SILVA: Then why do you giggle?

BABY DOLL: Can't help it. You make me feel kind of hysterical, Mr. Vacarro . . . Mr. Vacarro . . .

SILVA: Yes?

BABY DOLL [*a different attack, more feminine, pleading*]: I hope you don't think that Archie Lee was mixed up in that fire. I swear to goodness he never left the front porch. I remember it perfectly now. We just set here on the swing till the fire broke out and then we drove into town.

SILVA: To celebrate!

BABY DOLL: No, no, no!

SILVA: Twenty-seven wagons full of cotton's a pretty big piece of business to fall into your lap like a gift from the gods, Mrs. Meighan.

BABY DOLL: I thought you said we would drop the subject.

SILVA: You brought it up that time.

BABY DOLL: Well, please don't try to mix me up anymore, I swear to goodness the fire had already broke out when he got back.

SILVA: That's not what you told me a moment ago.

BABY DOLL: You got me all twisted up. We went in town. The fire broke out and we didn't know about it.

SILVA: I thought you said it irritated your sinus.

BABY DOLL: Oh my God, you sure put words in my mouth. Maybe I'd better make us some lemonade.

[*She starts to get up. Silva pulls her down.*]

What did you do that for?

SILVA: I don't want to be deprived of your company yet.

[*He lightly switches her legs with his crop.*]

61

BABY DOLL [*twisting*]: Mr. Vacarro, you're getting awfully familiar.

SILVA: Haven't you got any fun-loving spirit about you?

BABY DOLL: This isn't fun.

SILVA: Then why do you giggle?

BABY DOLL: I'm ticklish!

SILVA: Ticklish!

BABY DOLL: Yes, quit switching me, will you?

SILVA: I'm just shooing the flies off.

BABY DOLL: They don't hurt nothing. And would you mind moving your arm?

SILVA: Don't be so skittish!

BABY DOLL: All right! I'll get up then.

SILVA: Go on.

BABY DOLL [*trying*]: I feel so weak.

[*She pulls herself away from him.*]

Oh! My head's so buzzy.

SILVA: Fuzzy?

BABY DOLL: Fuzzy and buzzy. My head's swinging around. It's that swinging. . . . Is something on my arm?

62

SILVA: No.

BABY DOLL: Then what are you brushing?

SILVA: Sweat off. Let me wipe it. . . .

[*He brushes her arm with his handkerchief.*]

BABY DOLL [*laughing weakly*]: No, please don't. It feels funny.

SILVA: How does it feel?

BABY DOLL: Funny! All up and down. You cut it out now. If you don't cut it out I'm going to call.

SILVA: Call who?

BABY DOLL: That nigger who's cuttin' the grass across the road.

SILVA: Go on. Call then.

BABY DOLL: Hey!

[*Her voice is faint, weak.*]

Hey, boy, boy!

SILVA: Can't you call any louder?

BABY DOLL: I feel so funny! What's the matter with me?

SILVA: You're just relaxing. You're big. There's a lot of you and it's all relaxing! So give in. Stop getting yourself all excited.

BABY DOLL: I'm not—but you. . . .

63

SILVA: I!???

BABY DOLL: Yes. You. Suspicions. The ideas you have about my husband . . . suspicions.

SILVA: Suspicions? Such as . . .

BABY DOLL: Such as he burnt your gin down.

SILVA: Well?

BABY DOLL: He didn't.

SILVA: Didn't he?

BABY DOLL: I'm going inside. I'm going in the house.

[*She starts in. He follows close beside her.*]

SILVA: But you're afraid of the house! Do you believe in ghosts, Mrs. Meighan? I do. I believe in the presence of evil spirits.

BABY DOLL: What evil spirits you talking about now?

SILVA: Spirits of violence—and cunning—malevolence—cruelty—treachery—destruction. . . .

BABY DOLL: Oh, them's just human characteristics.

SILVA: They're evil spirits that haunt the human heart and take possession of it, and spread from one human heart to another human heart the way that a fire goes springing from leaf to leaf and branch to branch in a tree till a forest is all aflame with it—the birds take flight—the wild things are suffocated . . . everything green and beautiful is destroyed. . . .

64

BABY DOLL: You have got fire on the brain.

SILVA: I see it as more than it seems to be on the surface. I saw it last night as an explosion of those evil spirits that haunt the human heart—I fought it! I ran into it, beating it, stamping it, shouting the curse of God at it! They dragged me out, suffocating. I was defeated! When I came to, lying on the ground—the fire had won the battle, and all around was a ring of human figures! The fire lit their faces! I looked up. And they were illuminated! Their eyes, their teeth were SHINING!! SEE! LIKE THIS!

[*He twists his face into a grotesque grimace of pleasure. He holds her. They have arrived at the door to the interior of the house.*]

Yeah! Like this! Like this!!

[*He thrusts his grimacing face at her. She springs back, frightened.*]

BABY DOLL: Hey! Please! Don't do that! Don't scare me!

SILVA: The faces I saw—were grinning! Then I knew! I knew the fire was not accidental!

[*He holds her fast at the door.*]

BABY DOLL [*weakly*]: Not accidental?

SILVA: No, it was not accidental! It was an expression, a manifestation of the human will to *destroy*.

BABY DOLL: I wouldn't—feel that way—about it. . . .

SILVA: I do! I do! And so I say I believe in ghosts, in haunted places, places haunted by the people that occupy them with

65

hearts overrun by demons of hate and destruction. I believe his place, this house is haunted. . . . What's the matter?

BABY DOLL [*now thoroughly shaken*]: I don't know. . . .

SILVA: You're scared to enter the house, is that the trouble?

BABY DOLL [*calling*]: Aunt Rose. Aunt Rose!!

[*No answer.*]

That old woman can't hear a thing.

SILVA: There's no question about it. This place is haunted.

BABY DOLL: I'm getting—I'm getting so thirsty, so hot and thirsty!

SILVA: Then why don't you treat yourself to a drink of cold water?

BABY DOLL: I—I thought I might make us a—pitcher of—cold lemonade.

[*For some reason, Baby Doll doesn't want to enter the front door and she starts around the porch away from him. A board cracks under her weight. She screams, staggers. Silva rushes to her and seizes her plump arm, placing an arm behind her. She giggles weakly, but for the first time accepts his help.*]

BABY DOLL: The place is—collapsing right underneath me!

SILVA: You're trembling, Mrs. Meighan, shaking all over!

BABY DOLL: Your—your hands are so—hot—I don't think I ever felt hands as hot as your hands, they're—why they're like a couple of plates—took right out of—the oven!

66

SILVA: Burn, do they?

BABY DOLL: Yeah, they—*do*, they *burn*—me. . . .

SILVA: The idea of lemonade is very attractive. I would be glad to help you squeeze the lemons.

[*Tightens the pressure of his hands.*]

BABY DOLL: I know you would! I mean I—thanks, but—I can do it myself.

SILVA: You don't want my assistance, Mrs. Meighan?

BABY DOLL: Naw, it ain't necessary. . . .

SILVA: But then you would have to go into the house alone and the house is haunted! I better go in with you!

BABY DOLL: . . . No, it ain't necessary!

[*She is panting.*]

SILVA: You want me to stay on the porch?

BABY DOLL: Yeh, you stay on the porch!

SILVA: Why *shouldn't* I come inside?

BABY DOLL: No reason, just—just . . . !

[*She giggles weakly.*]

You stay out here while I make the lemonade and . . .

SILVA: All right. Go on, Mrs. Meighan. . . .

BABY DOLL: You stay out here. . . .

[*He doesn't answer. She stares at him, not moving.*]

SILVA: Now what's the matter now? Why don't you go in?

BABY DOLL: I don't think I better. I think I will go across the road to the gin. They got a water cooler. . . .

SILVA: The water cooler's for colored. A lady, a white lady like you, the wife of the big white boss, would place herself in an undignified position if she went over the road to drink with the hands! They might get notions about her! Unwholesome ideas! The sight of her soft white flesh, so smooth and abundant, might inflame their—natures . . .

[*Suddenly, Baby Doll sees something off and . . .*]

66] NEGRO BOY COMING DOWN THE ROAD.
He pushes a lawnmower. Behind him can be seen Archie Lee's gin, working.

67] BABY DOLL.
She rushes past Silva in the direction of the Negro boy, runs unsteadily as if she were drunk, across the unkempt lawn and out into the shimmering brilliance of the road.

BABY DOLL: Boy! Boy! I want you to cut my grass.

BOY: Can't now, ma'am.

BABY DOLL: Yes, you can.

BOY: I got a job cuttin' grass across Tiger Tail Bayou.

BABY DOLL: You cut grass here.

[*Her intensity frightens the boy.*]

68

BOY: Yes, ma'am, later.

BABY DOLL: NO! NOW! RIGHT NOW! I—I'll pay you five dollars. . . .

BOY: Yes, Ma'am.

BABY DOLL: I'll pay you five dollars . . . but *now*.

BOY [*scared to death*]: Yes ma'am. Yes ma'am.

BABY DOLL: And work close to the house. Hear! Speak up. Do you hear . . . ?

BOY: Yes ma'am. Yes ma'am.

[*Baby Doll sees* . . .]

68] SILVA.
As he comes into the picture, she retreats, walking backwards. Then there is a hoot from the gin. The sound from the gin suddenly stops. This calls her attention to the gin and she starts in that direction.

SILVA: Boy.

BOY: Yes, sir.

SILVA: Here's that five dollars the lady was mentioning.

BOY: Yes, sir.

SILVA: Only she don't want you to cut the grass.

BOY: Yes, sir.

SILVA: So you go on like you were. Understand?

69

BOY: Oh, yes, sir. Thank you, sir.

[*The boy, now completely bewildered, goes on, as he was.*]

69] INTERIOR. COTTON GIN.
Something is wrong. The men, including Rock, are gathered around a large piece of machinery. There is the characteristic debate as to what is wrong, opinions differing.

Onto this rather hectic group runs Baby Doll. Archie turns on her viciously.

ARCHIE: What're you doin' here, have you gone crazy??

BABY DOLL: I want to tell you something! You big slob.

[*This is just a little more than a desperate and harassed Archie can bear. He suddenly comes across and smacks Baby Doll. Good and hard!*]

ARCHIE: I told you never, never, never, to cross that road to this cotton gin—

70] CLOSE SHOT. SILVA.
He has entered and seen the action.

71] ARCHIE.
He notices Silva.

ARCHIE: . . . this cotton gin when niggers are working here.

BABY DOLL: You left me . . . you know what you left with me over there. . . .

[*Archie's eye wanders over to Silva, and Baby Doll sees him and clams up.*]

72] SILVA.

He now officially enters the scene.

SILVA: How's progress, Mr. Meighan?

ARCHIE: Fine! Great!

SILVA: Personally, I can't hear the gin at all.

BABY DOLL [*full of disgust*]: Big Shot!

[*And she exits.*]

SILVA: What's holding up?

ARCHIE: Nothing. . . .

SILVA: Rock!

[*Silva's own foreman steps forward.*]

ROCK: His saw-cylinder is busted.

SILVA: It figures. I inspected your equipment, Meighan, before I put in my own and I put up my own cotton gin because this equipment was rotten, was rotten, and still is rotten. Now it's quarter past two by my watch and I counted twenty-three fully loaded wagons still out on your runway. And if you can't move those wagons any faster . . .

ARCHIE: Now don't go into any hysterics. You Italians are prone to get too excited. . . .

SILVA: Never mind about we Italians. You better get yourself a new saw-cylinder and get this contraption running again. And if you can't get one in Clarksdale, you better go to Tunica, and if

71

you can't get one in Tunica, you better go to Memphis, and if you can't get one in Memphis, keep going to St. Louis. Now get on your horse.

ARCHIE: Now listen to me, Silva—

SILVA: One more crack out of you, I'm going to haul across the river. I said get on your horse.

[*Meighan hesitates. Then decides he must swallow this humiliation. There's nothing else for him to do under the circumstances. He exits.*]

[*Silva calls Rock over close.*]

SILVA [*sotto voce*]: I got a saw-cylinder in our commissary. Go get it and bring Hank over to help you put it in. Get this thing running. He ain't gonna get one in Clarksdale and if he goes to Memphis—well, don't wait for him.

[*And he exits.*]

73] ARCHIE LEE IN HIS CHEVY.
He nearly runs Baby Doll over.

BABY DOLL: Archie Lee! Archie Lee! Archie Lee!

[*She stumbles to her knees. She's sobbing. She rests a moment in the tall grass.*]

74] SILVA.
He runs up to her and stoops down to help her.

BABY DOLL: Le' me go. Le' me go.

[*She gets up and moves away from him towards her house.*]

75] AUNT ROSE COMFORT, AND BABY DOLL.
Aunt Rose comes out of the house all dressed up.

BABY DOLL: Aunt Rose Comfort.

[*Aunt Rose Comfort rushes past her.*]

Aunt Rose Comfort!! Where are you going?

AUNT ROSE: I have to see a sick friend at the county hospital.

[*And she is gone. Silva has caught up to Baby Doll again.*]

BABY DOLL: You might as well shout at the moon as that old woman.

SILVA: You didn't want her to go??

BABY DOLL: She's got no business leaving me here alone.

SILVA: It makes you uneasy to be alone here with me.

BABY DOLL: I think she just pretended not to hear me. She has a passion for chocolate candy and she watches the newspapers like a hawk to see if anybody she knows is registered at the county hospital.

SILVA: Hospital . . . ?

BABY DOLL: They give candy to patients at the county hospital, friends and relations send them flowers and candy and Aunt Rose Comfort calls on them and eats up their chocolate candy.

[*Silva explodes with laughter.*]

BABY DOLL: One time an old lady friend of Aunt Rose Comfort was dying at the county hospital and Aunt Rose Comfort went over and ate up a two-pound box of chocolate cherries while the old lady was dying, finished it all, hahahaha, while the old lady was dying.

[*They're both laughing together.*]

I like ole people—they're crazy. . . .

[*They both laugh together. . . .*]

SILVA: Mrs. Meighan. . . . May I ask you something? Of a personal nature?

BABY DOLL: What?

SILVA: Are you really married to Mr. Meighan?

BABY DOLL: Mr. Vacarro, that's a personal question.

SILVA: All questions are more or less personal, Mrs. Meighan.

BABY DOLL: Well, when I married I wasn't ready for marriage. I was still eighteen, but my daddy was practically on his death bed and wanted to see me took care of before he died. Well, ole Archie Lee had been hanging around like a sick dog for quite some time and . . . the boys are a sorry lot around here. Ask you to the movies and take you to the old rock quarry instead. You have to get out of the car and throw rocks at 'em, oh, I've had some experiences with boys that would curl your hair if I told you—some—experiences which I've had with boys!! But Archie Lee Meighan was an older fellow and in those days, well, his business was better. You hadn't put up that cotton gin of yours and Archie Lee was ginning out a lot of cotton. You remember?

SILVA: Yes, I remember. . . .

BABY DOLL: Well, I told my daddy I wasn't ready for marriage and my daddy told Archie Lee that I wasn't ready for it and he promised my daddy he'd wait till I was ready.

SILVA: Then the marriage was postponed?

BABY DOLL: Not the wedding, no, we had the wedding, my daddy gave me away. . . .

SILVA: But you said that Archie Lee waited?

BABY DOLL: Yes, *after* the wedding . . . he waited.

SILVA: For what?

BABY DOLL: For me to be ready for marriage.

SILVA: How long did he have to wait?

BABY DOLL: Oh, he's still waiting! Of course, we had an agreement that . . . well . . . I mean I told him that I'd be ready on my twentieth birthday—I mean ready or *not*. . . .

SILVA: And that's tomorrow?

BABY DOLL: Uh-huh.

SILVA: And are you . . . will you—be ready?

BABY DOLL: That all depends.

SILVA: What on?

BABY DOLL: Whether or not the furniture comes back—I guess. . . .

75

SILVA: Your husband sweats more than any man I know and now I understand why!!

[*There is a pause. They look at each other. Then Baby Doll looks away. Then with a sudden access of energy she enters the house, slams the screen door in his face and latches it.*]

BABY DOLL: *There now! You wait out here! You just wait out here!*

SILVA [*grinning at the screen door*]: Yes, ma'am. I will wait.

76] INTERIOR. DIMLY LIT ENTRANCE HALL OF MEIGHAN HOUSE.
Baby Doll turns from the screen door to the porch and stumbles along the vast and shadowy hall towards the dim light of the kitchen. As soon as she disappears, Vacarro is seen through the screen door. He jerks out a pocketknife and rips a hole in the screen.

Baby Doll calls anxiously, out of sight.

BABY DOLL [*from kitchen*]: *What's that?*

77] THE PORCH.
Vacarro whistles loudly and casually on the porch. He now slips his fingers through the hole and lifts the latch.

78] INTERIOR. KITCHEN OF MEIGHAN HOUSE. FULL SHOT.
Large, old-fashioned room with antiquated, but very capacious, equipment—large ice-box, large sinks and draining boards, large stove converted to gas.

Baby Doll stands in the middle of the floor with an apprehensive expression, but as Vacarro continues whistling on the porch, her usual placidity returns. She notices a kettle of greens on the stove.

76

BABY DOLL: Stupid old thing—forgot to light the stove.

[*She opens the ice-box for lemons.*]

Git me a Frigidaire one of these days.

[*The pan under the ice-box has overflowed and is swamping the floor.*]

Got to empty that pan.

[*Pulls it from under the ice-box with a grunt. A sound catches her ear, a sharp, slapping sound. She looks up anxiously, but the sound is not repeated. She takes out lemons, leaves the ice-box door hanging open. All her movements are fumbling and weak. She keeps rubbing her perspiring hands on her hips. She starts to cut a lemon, the knife slips and cuts her finger. She looks at the finger. It looks all right at first, then a drop of blood appears. She whimpers a little. The blood increases. She begins to cry like a baby.*]

[*She makes a vague, anxious movement. Again the slapping sound followed by a soft human sound like a chuckle. She looks that way. Cocks her head. But the sound is not repeated. Still squeezing the cut finger she begins to wander toward the front of the house.*]

CAMERA PANS WITH BABY DOLL AS SHE WANDERS THROUGH THE HOUSE.

[*She passes through a bare huge room with a dusty chandelier. It was the dining room when the house belonged to the old plantation owners. She whimpers under her breath, squeezing the bleeding finger. Now the blood is running down the hand to the wrist and down the wrist to the forearm and trickling into the soft hollow of her elbow. She groans and whimpers at the sight of the great flight of stairs, but starts up them.*]

77

[*Halfway up, at the landing, she hears the slapping sound again and the faunlike mocking laughter. She stops there and waits and listens—but the sound isn't immediately repeated, so she goes on up.*

[*She goes into the bathroom and starts to bandage her cut finger.*]

79] INTERIOR HALL OF MEIGHAN HOUSE. VA-CARRO DISCOVERED. FULL SHOT.
Vacarro is grinning up at the staircase. He slaps the banisters viciously with his whip, then chuckles.

CAMERA PANS WITH VACARRO.

[*He strolls into the kitchen, sees the ice-box door hanging open. Helps himself to the remains of a chicken, tearing it apart and gnawing the meat off it. He notices lemons and bloodspots— laughs.*]

SILVA: Trail o'blood! Ha ha!

[*He empties the flooded ice-pan over dirty dishes in sink.*]

Filth! Disgusting!

[*He slaps the wall with his whip and laughs.*]

80] INTERIOR. THE MEIGHANS' BEDROOM. BABY DOLL WANDERS IN FROM BATHROOM.
The finger is clumsily bandaged now, and she wanders across the room and examines herself in the mirror.

BABY DOLL: Look 'a' me! Big mess. . . .

[*There are dark stains of sweat on the watermelon pink dress. She lazily starts to remove it. Hears the slapping sound and laugh closer. Pauses, her mouth hanging open. Fumbling attempt to lock door. Key slips from her weak, nerveless fingers. She stoops, grunting, to pick it up.*]

81] INTERIOR KITCHEN. VACARRO SQUEEZING LEMONS AND HURLING THE RINDS SAVAGELY AWAY.

He finds gin bottle and sloshes gin into pitcher. Takes ice pick and chops off big hunk of ice. He seems to enjoy all these physical activities, grins tightly, exposing his teeth. Sticks ice pick into wall as if he were stabbing an enemy. Holds pitcher over his head whirling it rapidly so the drink sloshes over and ice rattles loudly, liquid running down his bare brown muscular arm. He drinks out of pitcher.

82] INTERIOR BEDROOM. BABY DOLL IN DAMP SLIP ROOTING IN CLOSET FOR A FRESH DRESS.

She hears ice rattling in pitcher. Pauses. Cocks head, listening apprehensively. Makes sure door is locked.

83] INTERIOR MEIGHANS' BEDROOM—A DIFFERENT ANGLE. BABY DOLL.

Her slip hangs half off one great globular breast, gleaming with sweat. She listens intently.

84] INTERIOR HALL AND STAIRWAY OF MEIGHAN HOUSE. VACARRO SOFTLY CLIMBING STAIRS. CAMERA FOLLOWS VACARRO INTO ROOMS ACROSS HALL FROM BEDROOM—THEN INTO CHILD'S NURSERY—

Never used. Hobby horse, small fenced bed, Mother Goose pictures on wall. He sits astride wooden horse, lashes its rump with the whip and rocks on it.

85] INTERIOR MEIGHANS' BEDROOM. BABY DOLL SPRINGS UP FROM FLOOR.

Baby Doll unlocks the door and peers anxiously into hall. The noise stops.

79

BABY DOLL: Archie Lee! Is that you?

[*Vacarro (out of sight) gives a soft wolf-whistle.*]

BABY DOLL: Who's that? Who's in there?

[*She crosses the hall into the nursery.*]

86] INTERIOR NURSERY. VACARRO SLIPPING INTO NEXT ROOM AS BABY DOLL ENTERS.

BABY DOLL [*nervously*]: Hey! What's goin' on?

[*Whip slap and soft mocking laughter, barely audible.*]

BABY DOLL: Mr. Vacarro? Are you in that room?

[*She crosses fearfully and enters the next room, Vacarro slipping out just before her entrance. Now she is really frightened.*]

87] INTERIOR EMPTY ROOM ADJOINING NURS-ERY—FULL SHOT. BABY DOLL ENTERS FEAR-FULLY.

BABY DOLL: You! Git outa my house! You got no right to come in! Where are you?

[*The door to the hall is locked. She hears the key turn in the lock. Gasps. Pounds door. Rushes back panting into nursery.*]

88] INTERIOR NURSERY. BABY DOLL RUSHES IN.

BABY DOLL: Mr. Vacarro, stop playing hide and seek!

[*The soft mocking laughter comes from the hall.*]

I know it's you! You're making me very nervous! Mr. Vacarro!! Mr. Vacarro. . . . Mr. Vacarro. . . .

[*With each call she creeps forward a few steps. All of a sudden he springs at her, shouting—*]

SILVA [*sudden shout*]: BOO!

[*At this point the scene turns into a wild romp of children. She shrieks with laughter. He howls, shouts. She shrieks with terror. She giggles hysterically, running into the hall and starting down steps.*

[*He leaps upon banister and slides to foot of stairs. She turns on the stairs and runs through various rooms slamming doors, giggling hysterically as she runs. A spirit of abandon enters the flight and the pursuit. As he follows her into the bedroom, she throws a pillow at him. He does a comic pratfall, embracing the pillow.*

[*She shrieks with laughter. He lunges toward her, throwing the pillow at her fugitive figure.*

[*She is about to run downstairs, but he blocks the way. She screams and takes the steps to the attic.*]

89] INTERIOR ATTIC.

Dusty late afternoon beams of light through tiny peaked windows in gables and a jumble of discarded things that have the poetry of things once lived with by the no-longer living.

Baby Doll doesn't stop to observe all this. She probably didn't even expect to find herself in an attic. She rushes in, slams the door, discovers a rusty bolt and bolts it just as Vacarro arrives at the door.

Her panting laughter expires as he pushes the door. She suddenly realizes the full import of her situation; gasps and backs away.

SILVA: Open Sesame!!

BABY DOLL [*in a low, serious voice*]: The game is over. I've quit.

SILVA: That's not fair, you've got to keep playing hide-and-seek till you're it.

BABY DOLL: Mr. Vacarro, will you please go back downstairs so I can unlock the door of this attic and come out—because the floor is weak. . . . I don't want to fall through. It's crumbling under my feet. I had no idea—I never been up here before!—it was in such a weaken condition.

[*There is something appealing in her soft, pleasing voice.*]

SILVA [*whispering, mouth to crack*]: I wouldn't dream of leaving you alone in a falling-down attic any more than you'd dream of eatin' a nut a man had cracked in his mouth. Don't you realize that??

BABY DOLL [*with sudden gathering panic*]: Mr. Vacarro! I got to get out of here. Quick! Go! Go!—down! Quick, please!

SILVA: I can hear that old floor giving away fast. . . .

BABY DOLL: So can I, and I'm *on* it.

SILVA: Shall I call the fire department to come here with a net to catch you when you fall through?

BABY DOLL: Wouldn't be time. No! Go! —then I can unlock the—

SILVA: No, I don't suppose they'd get here on time or if they did the net would be rotten as those fire hoses last night when they came to put out the fire that burned down my gin!

[*Suddenly, a piece of plaster falls beneath her feet. The rotten laths are exposed. She scrambles to another place, which is—or seems— equally shaky. She screams.*]

SILVA: Are you being attacked by a ghost in there?

BABY DOLL: Please be kind! Go away!

SILVA: Why don't you unlock the door so I can come to your rescue?

BABY DOLL: I—can't because . . .

SILVA: Huh? Huh?

BABY DOLL [*whisper*]: YOU.

[*Vacarro shoves door just a little with his shoulder. The bolt is not strong.*]

You . . . so! *Scare* me!

SILVA: Scared of *me??*

BABY DOLL: Yeah, scared of you and your—*whip.*

SILVA: Why're you scared of my whip? Huh? Do you think I might whip you? Huh? Scared I might whip you with it and

[*He slaps his boots regularly with the riding crop.*]

leave red marks on your—body, on your—creamy white silk— skin? Is that why're scared, Mrs. Meighan?

[*A murmur from her.*]

You want me to go away—with my whip??

83

[*Another murmur.*]

All right. Tell you what I'm gonna do. I'm gonna slip pencil and paper under this door and all I want is your signature on the paper. . . .

BABY DOLL: What paper?

SILVA: I guess that you would call it an affidavit, legally stating that Archie Lee Meighan burned down the Syndicate Gin. . . .

[*Pause.*]

Okay?

BABY DOLL: Mr. Vacarro, this whole floor's about to collapse under me!

SILVA: What do you say?

BABY DOLL: Just leave the paper, leave it right out there and I'll sign it and send it to you, I'll . . .

SILVA: Mrs. Meighan, I am a Sicilian. They're an old race of people, an ancient race, and ancient races aren't trustful races by nature. I've got to have the signed paper now. Otherwise I'm going to break this door down. Do you hear me?

[*A pause.*]

Do you hear me?

[*Silence.*

[*Whimpering, sobbing.*]

I gather you don't believe me.

[*Suddenly, with a single eloquent gesture of his whole body he has pushed the door open and on the other side Baby Doll, in absolute panic, runs, runs away from the threatening man and whip and towards the darkest corner of the attic. A few steps, however, and the floor really gives way. There is a shower of plaster, a rising cloud of plaster dust.*

[*Vacarro's face.*

[*The dust settles to reveal her, precariously perched across a beam . . .*

[*Vacarro calmly lights a cigarette.*]

SILVA: Now you're either going to agree to sign this thing, or I'm going to come out there after you and my additional weight will make the whole floor you know what!

BABY DOLL: OOOOOOH! What am I gonna do?

SILVA: Do what I tell you.

[*He gingerly steps on a place. . . . A trickle of plaster.*]

Awful bad shape.

[*He reaches and picks up a 1 x 3 about twelve feet long. On the end of it he puts a pencil and piece of paper.*]

BABY DOLL: O-o-o-o-h!

SILVA: What?

[*Suddenly, he stamps on the plaster. There is a big fall of plaster; Baby Doll screams.*]

85

BABY DOLL: All right, all right. —All right. . . . Hurry! Hurry!

SILVA: Hurry what?

BABY DOLL: I'll do whatever you want—only hurry!!

SILVA: Here it comes. . . .

[*He reaches out his little piece of paper and pencil, balanced on the 1 x 3. She grabs it, scribbles her name in frantic haste, panting, and puts the piece of paper back, fixing it on a nail on the end of the 1 x 3, and Vacarro pulls it back. He looks at her signature and throws back his head in a sudden wild laugh.*]

SILVA: Thank you. You may come out now.

BABY DOLL: Not till I hear you! Going down those stairs. . . .

SILVA [*grinning and starting down*]: Hear me? Hear my descending footsteps on the stairs. . . .

[*Vacarro straddles the long spiraled banister and slides all the way down to the landing at the bottom with a leap that starts another minor cascade.*

[*Baby Doll utters a little cry and comes out of the attic door. Silence. Putt-putt-putt-putt of the gin. She leans over stair well and looks straight down into the grinning face of Vacarro. He gives her a quick, grinning nod or salute.*]

SILVA: Okay, you're "Home free"! And so am I! Bye-bye!

BABY DOLL: Where are you going??

86

SILVA: Back to my little gray Quonset home in the West! For a peaceful siesta. . . .

BABY DOLL: Wait, please!—I want to—

[*She starts to come running down the stairs, her hair wild, panting, sweating, smeared with attic dust. Then halfway down she stops. . . .*]

BABY DOLL [*now stealing towards him*]: I want to—

[*But she can't remember what she "wants to." He waits quizzically with his cocky grin for her to complete her sentence but she doesn't. Instead she looks up and down him and her eyelids flutter as if the image could not be quietly contained.*]

[*He nods as if in agreement to something stated. He chuckles and then turns on his heels and starts briskly for the porch. She calls after him . . .*]

BABY DOLL: Was *that* all you wanted . . . ?

[*He turns and looks at her.*]

Me to confess that Archie Lee burnt down your gin?

SILVA: What else did you imagine?

[*She turns away like a shy child, serious-faced; she sits down on the bottom step.*]

SILVA [*gently*]: You're a child, Mrs. Meighan. That's why we played hide-and-seek, a game for children. . . .

BABY DOLL: You don't have to go all the way to your place for a nap. You could take a nap here.

87

SILVA: But all the furniture's been removed from the house.

BABY DOLL: Not the nursery stuff. They's a small bed in there, a crib, you could curl up and—let the slats down. . . .

[*An effect of two shy children trying to strike up a friendship. He continues to look at her. The windy afternoon has tossed a cloud over the sun, now declining. But it passes and his smile becomes as warm as sunlight. She isn't looking into his face but down at the scuffed kid slipper. Abruptly he gives a short quick nod and says simply . . .*]

SILVA: I'm happy to accept the invitation.

[*He starts up the stairs. When he gets to the point where she is sitting, he says*]:

Come up and sing me to sleep.

[*Then he continues on up.*

[*Baby Doll is left alone, bewildered, sitting on the big stair-case.*]

BABY DOLL [*to herself*]: My daddy would *turn* in his *grave*.

[*She starts up the stairs. . . .*]

90] THE NURSERY.
Vacarro is on the crib, with the slats down. He is curled with his thumb in his mouth. She comes to view, stands in the doorway a moment, then goes and crouches beside the bed. Gently, she raises his head and bare throat, crooks an arm under and begins to sing: "Rock-a-Bye Baby."

He sighs contentedly, removes the signed paper from his shirt pocket and tucks it under his belt for safer keeping.

Then he appears to fall asleep.

DISSOLVE.

91] IN A HOSPITAL ROOM.

Aunt Rose Comfort is sitting by a friend who is in her death coma.
Aunt Rose eating chocolate cherries.

DISSOLVE.

92] SUPPLY STORE IN MEMPHIS. MEIGHAN AT COUNTER.

ARCHIE [*to Clerk*]: Godamighty man, I'm good for it.

[*He reaches for the part he has come for. It's wrapped and ready to go.*]

CLERK: We have orders. No credit. Cash basis. Everything.

ARCHIE: I warn you. I'll never come in this store again.

CLERK: Sorry.

ARCHIE: Look, I just happened to leave the place in my work clothes. My wallet ain't on me!

CLERK: Cash only.

[*Mr. Archie Lee Meighan suddenly turns and leaves in complete disgust.*]

93] FRONT. ARCHIE LEE'S GIN.

It is several hours later and he has driven back from Memphis. He halts his motor with an exhausted grunt. He appears to have shrunk in size. He carries a sweat-drenched coat over his arm and the sweaty shirt clings to him. His chest heaves with unhealthy fast respiration, and he fingers the unbuttoned collar, as he takes in the

89

*situation: The gin is running again!!!—and without his O.K. —
and how did they get the damned thing going again!!??*

93A] INTERIOR GIN.
He walks in and passes Rock.

ARCHIE: Hahaha! Looks like we're back in business.

ROCK [*offering him only the most fleeting glance*]: Does, doesn't
it.

ARCHIE: You all must have done some mighty fast repairs.

ROCK: No repairs—put in a new saw-cylinder.

ARCHIE: From where? Out of a cloud? Why, I checked every
supply outfit between Memphis and Greenville and nobody's
got a new saw-cylinder ready for installation before next
Wednesday.

ROCK [*tersely*]: Boss had one at our place. I put it in.

ARCHIE: How do you like that? How come I wasn't let in on
this piece of information before I lit out of here on the wild-
goose chase that just about killed me? Where is that wop
Vacarro? I want to get some explanation of this.

[*At this precise moment the whistle blows, announcing the end of
the day and the gin machinery stops work. The Negroes, who have
been working as porters and mechanics, line up for pay.*]

ROCK [*meantime*]: You seen the boss-man, Norm?

[*A Negro shakes his head.*

[*Rock notices Archie looking at the line a little worried.*]

ROCK [*to Archie*]: Don't worry. Vacarro is meeting the payroll for tonight.

ARCHIE: Where is he?

ROCK [*to another Negro*]: Moose, you seen the boss?

MOOSE: No time lately, Capt'n.

94] THE GIN. (ANOTHER ANGLE)
Meighan retreats from the gin uncertainly. Camera follows.

Halfway across the road he hears laughter, evidently directed at him. His back stiffens. Something has happened, he feels, that has somehow made him the patsy of whatever occasion this is.

95] CLOSE SHOT. MEIGHAN.
Suspicious, angry, something violent and dangerous is growing up in his heart. He mutters to himself. Hears the laughter again. Curses to himself.

96] MEIGHAN ENTERS THE BIG FRONT YARD AND STARES AT THE HOUSE.

97] THE HOUSE.
Silent. Not a move. Not a sound.

98] MEIGHAN NOTICES VACARRO'S DISCARDED SHIRT.
He picks it up and lifts his head and calls into the house.

ARCHIE: Hey! Anybody living here? Anybody still living in this house?

99] UPSTAIRS. THE NURSERY.

Baby Doll, considerably disarrayed, has heard Archie's shout from below and is just making her way on hands and knees to the window. Now she crawls on the floor over to the crib.

BABY DOLL: It's Archie Lee.

[*Downstairs screen door slams. Vacarro gurgles, murmurs, whimpers, all of which mean "don't bother me, I want to sleep."*

[*There is a sudden shout from downstairs as if a cry of pain.*]

100] DOWNSTAIRS.
What Meighan sees is the debris of the ceiling. He looks up at the gaping hole in the roof over his head at the top of the stair well and down the stairs. Baby Doll appears on the staircase in a silken wrapper.

ARCHIE: *What happened here?*

[*Baby Doll doesn't answer. She stares at him with blank insolence.*]

ARCHIE: Hunh? I said what the hell happened here?

BABY DOLL: You mean that mess in the hall? The plaster broke in the attic.

ARCHIE: How'd that—how'd that—happen?

BABY DOLL: How does anything happen? It just happened.

[*She comes on lazily down, avoiding his look.*]

101] INTERIOR NIGHT. DOWNSTAIRS. FRONT HALL.

ARCHIE: Ain't I told you not to slop around here in a slip?

92

[*She gives a faint indifferent shrug which enrages him; he senses something openly contemptuous, a change in her attitude towards him. He grabs her bare shoulder.*]

What's the matter with your skin? It looks all broke out.

[*Inspects the inflamed welts.*]

What's this?

BABY DOLL: What's what?

ARCHIE: These marks on you?

BABY DOLL: Mosquito bites, I scratched them. . . . Lemme go.

ARCHIE [*bellowing*]: Ain't I told you not to slop around here in a slip???!!!

[*Aunt Rose Comfort, alarmed by the shout, appears in door to kitchen, crying out thin and high.*]

AUNT ROSE: Almost ready, now, folks, almost ready!!

[*She rushes back into the kitchen with her frightened cackle. There is a crash of china from the kitchen.*]

ARCHIE: The breakage alone in that kitchen would ruin a well-to-do man! Now you go up and git some decent clo'se on yuh an' come back down. Y'know they got a new bureau in Washington, D.C. It's called the U.W. Bureau. Y'know what U.W. stands for? It stands fo' useless women. They's secret plans on foot to round 'em all up and shoot 'em. Hahahaha!

93

BABY DOLL: How about men that's destructive? Don't they have secret plans to round up men that's destructive and shoot them too?

ARCHIE: What destructive men you talkin' about?

BABY DOLL: Men that blow things up and burn things down because they're too evil and stupid to git along otherwise. Because fair competition is too much for 'em. So they turn criminal. Do things like arson. Willful destruction of property by fire. . . .

[*She steps out on the porch. Night sounds. A cool breeze tosses her damp curls. She sniffs the night air like a young horse. . . .*

[*The porch light, a milky globe patterned with dead insects, turns on directly over her head and Archie Lee comes up behind her and grips her bare shoulders, his face anxious, cunning.*]

ARCHIE: Who said that to you? Where'd you git that from??

BABY DOLL: Turn that porch light off. There's men on the road can see me.

ARCHIE: Who said *arson* to you? Who spoke of willful destruction of . . . YOU never knew them words. Who SAID 'em to yuh?

BABY DOLL: Sometimes, Big Shot, you don't seem t' give me credit for much intelligence! I've been to school, in my life, and I'm a—magazine reader!

[*She shakes off his grip and starts down porch steps. There is a group of men on Tiger Tail Road. One of them gives a wolf-whistle. At once, Archie Lee charges down the steps and across the yard towards the road—crying out—*]

94

ARCHIE: *Who gave that whistle??* Which of you give a wolf-whistle at my wife?

[*The group ignores him except for a light mocking laugh as they continue down the road. The camera returns to Baby Doll blandly smiling.*

[*We hear the rattle of the cistern pump being vigorously exercised in the side yard. Archie Lee stalks back up to the porch, winded, like an old hound. . . .*]

ARCHIE: Men from the Syndicate *Plantation! White an' black* mixed! Headed fo' Tiger Tail Bayou with frog gigs and rubber boots on! I just hope they turn downstream and trespass across my property! I just hope they dast to! I'll blast them out of the Bayou with a shotgun!

BABY DOLL: Small dogs have a loud bark.

ARCHIE: Nobody's gonna insult no woman of *mine!!*

BABY DOLL: You take a lot for granted when you say *mine.* This afternoon I come to you for protection. What did I *git? Slapped!* And told to go home. . . . I, for one, have got no sympathy for you, now or ever. An' the rasslin' match between us is *over* so let me *go!*

ARCHIE: You're darn tootin' it's over. In just three hours the terms of the agreement will be settled for good.

BABY DOLL: Don't count on it. That agreement is canceled. Because it takes two sides to make an agreement, like an argument, and both sides got to live up to it completely. You didn't live up to yours. Stuck me in a house which is haunted and five complete sets of unpaid-for furniture was removed from it las' night, OOHH I'm *free* from my side of that bargain!

95

ARCHIE: *Sharp at midnight!* We'll find out about that.

BABY DOLL: Too much has happened here lately. . . .

[*She descends into yard. Archie Lee eyes her figure, sweating, licking his chops.*]

ARCHIE: Well . . . my credit's wide open again!

BABY DOLL: So is the jailhouse door wide open for you if the truth comes out.

ARCHIE: You threatenin' me with—*blackmail??*

BABY DOLL: Somebody's drawin' some cool well water from the pump back there.

[*She starts back. He follows. The full frog-gigging moon emerges from a mackerel sky, and we see Vacarro making his ablutions at the cistern pump with the zest and vigor of a man satisfied.*]

BABY DOLL [*with unaccustomed hilarity*]: HEIGH-HO SIL-VER . . . HaHa!!

[*Archie Lee stops dead in his tracks.*]

ARCHIE: Him?! Still on the place?

BABY DOLL: Give me another drink of that sweet well water, will yuh, Mistuh Vaccaro? You're the first person could draw it.

ARCHIE [*advancing*]: YOU STILL HERE?

BABY DOLL: Archie Lee, Mr. Vacarro says he might not put up a new cotton gin, but let you gin cotton for him all the time, now. Ain't you pleased about that? Tomorrow he plans to come with lots more cotton, maybe another twenty-seven wagon-loads. And while you're ginning it out, he'll have me to entertain him, make lemonade for him. It's going to go on and on! Maybe even next fall.

SILVA [*through the water*]: Good neighbor policy in practice.

[*Having wetted himself down he now drinks from the gourd.*]

I love well water. It tastes as fresh as if it never was tasted before. Mrs. Meighan, would you care for some, too?

BABY DOLL: Why thank you, yes, I would.

[*There is a grace and sweetness and softness of speech about her, unknown before. . . .*]

SILVA: Cooler nights have begun.

[*Archie Lee has been regarding the situation, with its various possibilities, and is far from content.*]

ARCHIE: How long you been on the place?

SILVA [*drawling sensuously with eyes on girl*]: All this unusually long hot fall afternoon I've imposed on your hospitality. You want some of this well water?

ARCHIE [*with a violent gesture of refusal*]: Where you been here???

SILVA: Taking a nap on your only remaining bed. The crib in the nursery with the slats let down. I had to curl up on it like a pretzel, but the fire last night deprived me of so much sleep that almost any flat surface was suitable for slumber.

[*Winks impertinently at Archie Lee, then turns to grin sweetly at Baby Doll, wiping the drippings of well water from his throat. Then turns back to Archie.*]

But there's something sad about it. Know what I mean?

ARCHIE: Sad about what??

SILVA: An unoccupied nursery in a house, and all the other rooms empty. . . .

ARCHIE: That's no problem of yours!

SILVA: The good neighbor policy makes your problems mine—and vice versa. . . .

AUNT ROSE [*violent and high and shrill, from the back steps*]: SUPPER! READY! CHILDREN. . . .

[*She staggers back in.*

[*Now there's a pause in which all three stand tense and silent about the water pump. Baby Doll with her slow, new smile speaks up first. . . .*]

BABY DOLL: You all didn't hear us called in to supper?

ARCHIE: You gonna eat here tonight?

SILVA: Mrs. Meighan asked me to stay for supper but I told her I'd better get to hear the invitation from the head of the house before I'd feel free to accept it. So . . . What do you say?

98

[*A tense pause . . . then, with great difficulty . . .*]

ARCHIE: Stay! . . . fo' supper.

BABY DOLL: You'll have to take potluck.

SILVA: I wouldn't be putting you out?

[*This is addressed to Baby Doll, who smiles vaguely and starts toward the house, saying . . .*]

BABY DOLL: I better get into mu' clo'se. . . .

ARCHIE: Yeah . . . hunh. . . .

[*They follow her sensuous departure with their eyes till she fades into the dusk.*]

ARCHIE: Did I understand you to say you wouldn't build a new gin but would leave your business to me?

SILVA: If that's agreeable with you. . . .

ARCHIE [*turning from his wife's back to Vacarro's face*]: I don't know yet, I'll have to consider the matter. . . . Financing is involved such as—new equipment. . . . Let's go in and eat now. I got a pain in my belly, I got a sort of heartburn. . . .

102] INTERIOR. HOUSE.
They enter the kitchen and then to the dining room. Archie Lee's condition is almost shock. He can't quite get with the situation. He numbly figures that he'd better play it cool till the inner fog clears. But his instinct is murder. His cowardly caution focuses his malice on the old woman and the unsatisfactory supper she's prepared.

ARCHIE: Hey! Hey! One more place at the table! Mr. Vacarro from the Syndicate Plantation is stayin' to supper.

AUNT ROSE [*with a startled outcry, clutching her chest*]: Oh—I had no idea that company was expected. Just let me—change the silver and . . .

ARCHIE: Another place is all that's called for. Have you been here all day?

AUNT ROSE: What was that, Archie Lee?

ARCHIE: HAVE YOU BEEN IN THE HOUSE ALL AFTERNOON OR DID YOU LIGHT OUT TO THE COUNTY HOSPITAL TO EAT SOME CHOCOLATE CANDY????

[*Aunt Rose gasps as if struck, then she cackles . . .*]

AUNT ROSE: I—I—visited!—an old friend in a—coma!

ARCHIE: Then you was out while I was—.

[*He turns to Vacarro—fiercely.*]

I work like the hammers of hell! I come home to find the attic floor has fell through, my wife bad-tempered, insulting! and a supper of hog slops—. Sit down, eat. I got to make a phone call.

[*He crosses somewhat unsteadily into the hall and picks up the telephone as Baby Doll descends the grand staircase and goes past him with face austerely averted. She is clad in a fresh silk sheath and is adjusting an earring as she passes through the hall. We go with her into the dining room.*]

BABY DOLL: He's at the phone about something and if I was you, I wouldn't hang around long.

SILVA: I think I've got the ace of spades in my pocket.

[*He pats where he's stashed the confession by Baby Doll.*]

BABY DOLL: Don't count on a law court. Justice is deaf and blind as that old woman!

[*Aunt Rose Comfort rushes out to cut roses for a vase to set on the table.*]

BABY DOLL: I'm advising you, go! —while he's on the phone.

SILVA: I find you different this evening in some way.

BABY DOLL: Never mind, just go! Before he gits off the phone.

SILVA: Suddenly grown up!

BABY DOLL [*looking at him gratefully*]: I feel cool and rested, for the first time in my life. I feel that way, rested and cool.

[*A pause.*]

Are you going or staying???

[*They are close together by table. Suddenly she catches her breath and flattens her body to his. The embrace is active. She reaches above her and pulls the beaded chain of the light, plunging the room in dark. We hear two things: The breath of the embracing couple and the voice of Archie Lee on the phone.*]

ARCHIE: A bunch of men from the Syndicate Plantation are out frog-giggin' on Tiger Tail Bayou and I thought we all might join the party. How's about meeting at the Brite Spot in halfn hour? With full equipment.

[*A few more indistinct words, he hangs up. The light is switched back on in the dining room. Aunt Rose rushes in.*]

101

AUNT ROSE: Roses! Poems of nature . . .

[*Archie Lee enters from the hall. His agitation is steadily mounting.*]

ARCHIE: Never mind poems of nature, just put food on th' table!

AUNT ROSE: If I'd only known that company was expected, I'd . . .

[*Her breathless voice expires as she scuttles about putting roses in a vase.*]

AUNT ROSE: Only take a minute.

ARCHIE: We ain't waitin' no minute. Bring out the food. . . .

[*Baby Doll smiles, rather scornfully, at Archie Lee bullying the old woman.*]

ARCHIE: Is that what they call a Mona Lisa smile you got on your puss?

BABY DOLL: Don't pick on Aunt Rose. . . .

ARCHIE [*shouting*]: Put some food on the table!! [*Then muttering dangerously.*] I'm going to have a talk with that old woman, right here tonight. She's outstayed her welcome.

SILVA: What a pretty blue wrapper you're wearing tonight, Mrs. Meighan.

BABY DOLL [*coyly*]: Thank you, Mr. Vacarro.

SILVA: There's so many shades of blue. Which shade is that?

102

BABY DOLL: Just baby blue.

ARCHIE: Baby blue, huh!

SILVA: It brings out the blue of your eyes.

ARCHIE [*screaming*]: Food! Food!

AUNT ROSE: Immediately! This instant!

[*She comes through the door from the kitchen, holding a big plate of greens, which she sets on the table with great apprehension. They are not really cooked. Archie stares at them.*]

103] CLOSE SHOT OF GREENS, WHICH ARE ALMOST RAW.

104] CLOSE SHOT OF ARCHIE SWEARING UNDER HIS BREATH.

105] GROUP SCENE.

BABY DOLL: This wrapper was part of my trousseau, as a matter of fact. I got all my trousseau at Memphis at various departments where my daddy was known. Big department stores on Main Street.

ARCHIE: WHAT IS THIS STUFF??!! GRASS??!!

BABY DOLL: Greens! Don't you know greens when you see them?

ARCHIE: This stuff is greens?!!

[*Aunt Rose comes nervously from the pantry.*]

AUNT ROSE: Archie Lee dotes on greens, don't you, Archie Lee?

103

ARCHIE: No, I don't.

AUNT ROSE: You don't? You don't dote on greens?

ARCHIE: I don't think I ever declared any terrible fondness for greens in your presence.

AUNT ROSE: Well, somebody did.

ARCHIE: Somebody did—sometime, somewhere, but that don't mean it was me!

[*He lurches back in his chair and half rises, swinging to face Vacarro—who has taken Baby Doll's hand under the table.*

[*Vacarro smiles blandly.*]

BABY DOLL: Sit back down, Big Shot, an' eat your greens. Greens puts iron in the system.

AUNT ROSE: I thought that Archie Lee doted on greens! — All those likes and dislikes are hard to keep straight in your head. But Archie Lee's easy to cook for. Jim's a complainer, oh, my, what a complainer Jim is, and Susie's household, they're nothing but complainers.

ARCHIE: *Take this slop off th' table!!*

AUNT ROSE [*terrified*]: I'll—cook you some—eggs Birmingham! —These greens didn' cook long enough. I played a fool trick with my stove. I forgot to light it! Ha ha! When I went to the store—I had my greens on the stove. I thought I'd left 'em boilin'. But when I got home I discovered that my stove wasn't lighted.

ARCHIE: Why do you say "my" stove? Why is everything "my"?

BABY DOLL: Archie Lee, I believe you been drinkin'!

ARCHIE: You keep out of this! Set down, Aunt Rose.

AUNT ROSE: —Do what, Archie Lee?

ARCHIE: Set down here. I want to ask you a question.

[*Aunt Rose sits down slowly and stiffly, all atremble.*]

What sort of—plans have you made?

AUNT ROSE: Plans, Archie Lee? What sort of plans do you mean?

ARCHIE: Plans for the future!

BABY DOLL: I don't think this kind of discussion is necessary in front of company.

SILVA: Mr. Meighan, when a man is feeling uncomfortable over something, it often happens that he takes out his annoyance on some completely innocent person just because he has to make somebody suffer.

ARCHIE: You keep outa this, too. I'm askin' Aunt Rose a perfectly sensible question. Now, Aunt Rose. You been here since August and that's a mighty long stay. Now, it's my honest opinion that you're in need of a rest. You been cookin' around here and cookin' around there for how long now? How long have you been cookin' around people's houses?

AUNT ROSE [*barely able to speak*]: I've helped out my—relatives, my—folks—whenever they—*needed me to!* I was always—*invited!* Sometimes—*begged* to come! When *babies* were expected or when somebody was *sick*, they called for Aunt

105

Rose, and Aunt Rose was always—ready. . . . Nobody *ever* had to—*put me—out!* —If you—gentlemen will excuse me from the table—I will pack my things! If I hurry I'll catch the nine o'clock bus to—

[*She can't think "where to." Vacarro seizes her hand, pushing back from table.*]

SILVA: Miss Rose Comfort. Wait. I'll drive you home.

AUNT ROSE: —I don't!—have nowhere to!—go. . . .

SILVA: Yes, you do. I need someone to cook for me at my place. I'm tired of my own cooking and I am anxious to try those eggs Birmingham you mentioned. Is it a deal?

AUNT ROSE: —Why, I—

BABY DOLL: Sure it's a deal. Mr. Vacarro will be good to you, Aunt Rose Comfort, and he will even *pay* you, and maybe— well—y'never can tell about things in the future. . . .

AUNT ROSE: *I'll run pack my things!*

[*She resumes reedy hymn in a breathless, cracked voice as she goes upstairs.*]

ARCHIE: Anything else around here you wanta take with yuh, Vacarro?

[*Vacarro looks around coolly as if considering the question. Baby Doll utters a high, childish giggle.*]

Well, *is* they? Anything else around here you wanta take away with yuh?

106

BABY DOLL [*rising gaily*]: Why, yaiss, Archie Lee. Mr. Vacarro noticed the house was overloaded with furniture and he would like us to loan him five complete sets of it to—

ARCHIE [*seizing neck of whiskey bottle*]: YOU SHUDDUP! I will git to you later.

BABY DOLL: If you ever git to me it sure is going to be *later*, ha ha, *much* later, ha ha!

[*She crosses to kitchen sink, arranging her kiss-me-quicks in the soap-splashed mirror, also regarding the two men behind her with bland satisfaction: her childish face, beaming, is distorted by the flawed glass.*

[*She sings or hums "Sweet and Lovely." Archie Lee stands by table, breathing heavy as a walrus in labor. He looks from one to the other. Silva coolly picks up a big kitchen knife and lops off a hunk of bread, then tosses kitchen knife out of Archie Lee's reach and then he dips bread in pot of greens.*]

SILVA: Colored folks call this pot liquor.

BABY DOLL: I love pot liquor.

SILVA: Me, too.

BABY DOLL [*dreamily*]: —Crazy 'bout pot liquor. . . .

[*She turns about and rests her hips against sink. Archie Lee's breathing is loud as a cotton gin, his face fiery. He takes swallow after swallow from bottle.*

[*Vacarro devours bread.*]

SILVA: Mm-*UMMM!*

107

BABY DOLL: Good?

SILVA: *Yes!—Good!*

BABY DOLL: *—That's* good. . . .

[*Old Fussy makes a slow stately entrance, pushing the door open wider with her fat hips and squawking peevishly at this slight inconvenience.*

[*Meighan wheels about violently and hurls the empty bottle at her. She flaps and squawks back out. Her distressed outcries are taken up by her sisters, who are sensibly roosting.*]

BABY DOLL [*giggling*]: Law! Ole Fussy mighty near made it that time! Why, that old hen was comin' in like she'd been invited t'supper.

[*Her giggly voice expires as Meighan wheels back around and bellows.*

[*Archie Lee explodes volcanically. His violence should give him almost a Dostoevskian stature.*

[*It builds steadily through the scene as a virtual lunacy possesses him with the realization of his hopeless position.*]

ARCHIE: *OH HO HO HO HO!*

[*He kicks the kitchen door shut.*]

Now you all listen to me! Quit giving looks back an' forth an' listen to me! Y'think I'm deaf, dumb an' blind or somethin', do yuh? You're *mistook*, Oh, brother, but you're much, much—*mistook!* Ohhhh, I knooow! —I guess I look like a—I guess I look like a—

108

[*Panting, puffing pause; he reels a little, clutching chair back.*]

BABY DOLL [*insolently childish lisp*]: What d'you guess you look like, Archie Lee? Y'was about t' tell us an' then yuh quit fo' some—

ARCHIE: *Yeah, yeah, yeah!* Some little innocent Baby Doll of a wife not ready fo' marriage, oh, no, not yet ready for marriage but plenty ready t'— Oh, I see how it's funny, I can see how it's funny, I see the funny side of it. *Oh ho ho ho ho!* Yes, it sure is comic, comic as hell! But there's one little *teensy-eensy* little— thing that you—*overlooked!* I! Got *position!* Yeah, yeah, *I* got *position!* Here in this county! Where I was bo'n an' brought up! I hold a respected position, lifelong!—member of— Wait! Wait!—Baby Doll. . . .

[*She had started to cross past him; he seizes her wrist. She wrenches free. Vacarro stirs and tenses slightly but doesn't rise or change his cool smile.*]

On my side 're friends, long-standin' *bus'ness* associates, an' *social!* See what I mean? You ain't got that advantage, have you, mister? Huh, mister? Ain't you a dago, or something, excuse me, I mean Eyetalian or something, here in Tiger Tail County?

SILVA: Meighan, I'm not a doctor, but I was a medical corpsman in the Navy and you've got a very unhealthy looking flush on your face right now which is almost purple as a—

[*He was going to say "baboon's behind."*]

ARCHIE [*bellowing out*]: ALL I GOT TO DO IS GIT ON THAT PHONE IN THE HALL!

SILVA: And call an ambulance from the county hospital?

109

ARCHIE: Hell, I don't even need t' make a phone call! I can handle this situation *m'self!*—with legal protection that no one could—

SILVA [*still coolly*]: What situation do you mean, Meighan?

ARCHIE: Situation which I come home to find here under my roof! Oh, I'm not such a marble-missing old fool! —I couldn't size it up! —I sized it up the moment I seen you was still on this place and *her!*—with that *sly smile on her!*

[*Takes a great swallow of liquor from the fresh bottle.*]

And *you* with *yours* on *you!* I know how to wipe off both of those sly—!

[*He crosses to the closet door. Baby Doll utters a gasp and signals Vacarro to watch out.*

[*Vacarro rises calmly.*]

SILVA: Meighan?

[*He speaks coolly, almost with a note of sympathy.*]

You know, and *I* know, and I *know* that you *know* that I *know!*— That you set fire to my cotton gin last night. You burnt down the Syndicate Gin and I got in my pocket a signed affidavit, a paper, signed by a witness, whose testimony will even hold up in the law courts of Tiger Tail County! —That's all I come here for and that's all I got . . . whatever else you suspect—well!— you're mistaken. . . . Isn't that so, Mrs.Meighan? Isn't your husband mistaken in thinking that I got anything out of this place but this signed affidavit which was the purpose of my all-afternoon call?

110

[*She looks at him, angry, hurt.*

[*Meighan wheels about, panting.*]

SILVA [*continuing*]: Yes, I'm foreign but I'm not revengeful, Meighan, at least not more than is rightful.

[*Smiles sweetly.*]

—I think we got a workable good neighbor policy between us. It might work out, anyhow I think it deserves a try. Now as to the other side of the situation, which I don't have to mention. Well, all I can say is, a certain attraction—exists! Mutually, I believe! But nothing's been rushed. I needed a little shut-eye after last night's—excitement. I took a nap upstairs in the nursery crib with the slats let down to accommodate my fairly small frame, and I have faint recollection of being sung to by someone—a lullaby song that was—sweet . . .

[*His voice is low, caressing.*]

—and the touch of—cool fingers, but that's all, absolutely!

ARCHIE: Y'think I'm gonna put up with this—?

SILVA: Situation? You went to a whole lot of risk an' trouble to get my business back. Now don't you want it? It's up to you, Archie Lee, it's—

ARCHIE: COOL! Yeah, cool, very cool!

SILVA: —The heat of the fire's died down. . . .

ARCHIE: UH—HUH! YOU'VE FIXED YOUR WAGON! WITH THIS SMART TALK, YOU JUST NOW FIXED YOUR WAGON! I'M GONNA MAKE A PHONE CALL

111

THAT'LL WIPE THE GRIN OFF YOUR GREASY WOP FACE FOR GOOD!

[*He charges into hall and seizes phone.*]

SILVA [*crossing to Baby Doll at kitchen sink*]: Is my wop face greasy, Mrs. Meighan?

[*She remains at mirror but her childish smile fades: her face goes vacant and blind: she suddenly tilts her head back against the bare throat of the man standing behind her. Her eyes clenched shut. . . .*]

[*His eyelids flutter as his body presses against all the mindless virgin softness of her abundant young flesh. We can't see their hands, but hers are stretched behind her, his before him.*]

106] HALL.

ARCHIE [*bellowing like a steer*]: I WANT SPOT, MIZZ HOPKINS, WHE' IS SPOT!?

107] BABY DOLL WITH VACARRO.

BABY DOLL: I think you better go 'way. . . .

SILVA: I'm just waiting to take you girls away with me. . . .

BABY DOLL [*softly as in a dream*]: Yeah. I'm goin' too. I'll check in at the Kotton King Hotel and— Now I better go up an'— he'p Aunt Rose Comfo't pack. . . .

[*Releases herself regretfully from the embrace and crosses into hall.*]

108] HALL. CLOSE SHOT OF SILVA LOOKING AFTER HER. IN THE HALL SHE UTTERS A SHARP OUT- CRY AS MEIGHAN STRIKES AT HER.

BABY DOLL: YOU GONNA BE SORRY FOR EV'RY TIME YOU LAID YOUR UGLY OLE HANDS ON ME, YOU STINKER, YOU! YOU STINKING STINKER, STINKERRR!

[*Her footsteps running upstairs. Vacarro chuckles almost silently and goes quietly out the back door.*]

109] THE YARD.
Vacarro crosses through a yard littered with uncollected garbage, tin cans, refuse. . . .

110] HALL. MEIGHAN REMOVES SHOTGUN FROM CLOSET.

111] YARD. CUT BACK TO EXTERIOR.
Crooked moon beams fitfully through a racing mackerel sky, the air's full of motion.

Vacarro picks his way fastidiously among the refuse, wades through the tall seeding grass, into the front yard. Clutches the lower branch of a pecan tree and swings up into it. Cracks a nut between his teeth as—

ARCHIE [*shouting and blundering through the house*]: HEY! WHERE YOU HIDING? WHERE YOU HIDING, WOP?!

112] HOUSE. CLOSE SHOT OF MEIGHAN WITH SHOTGUN AND LIQUOR BOTTLE, ALREADY STUMBLING DRUNK. . . .

113] YARD. EXTERIOR NIGHT. VACARRO IN TREE. VOICE OF BABY DOLL AT PHONE.

BABY DOLL: I want the Police Chief. Yes, the Chief, not just the police, the Chief. This is Baby Doll McCorkle speaking, the ex-Mrs. Meighan on Tiger Tail Road! My husband has got a shotgun and is threat'nin to—

[*Her voice turns into a scream. She comes running out front door followed by Meighan. She darts around side of house. Meighan is very drunk now. He goes the opposite way around the house. Vacarro drops out of tree and gives Baby Doll a low whistle. She rushes back to front yard.*]

BABY DOLL: *Oh, Gah, Gah, watch out, he's got a shotgun. He's— crazy! I callt th' Chief of—*

[*Vacarro leaps into tree again.*]

SILVA: Grab my hand! Quick! Now *up! Up*, now Baby Doll!

[*He hoists her into tree with him as the wild-eyed old bull comes charging back around house with his weapon. He blasts away at a shadow. (The yard is full of windy shadows.) He is sobbing.*]

ARCHIE: BABY DOLL! BABY! BABY! BABY DOLL! MY BABY!

[*He goes stumbling around back of house, great wind in the trees. Baby Doll rests in the arms of Vacarro.*

[*Meighan in back yard. Storm cellar door bangs open. Meighan fires through it. Then at chicken coop. Then into wheelless limousine chassis in side yard, etc., etc.*

[*Shot of Vacarro and Baby Doll in fork of pecan tree.*]

SILVA [*grinning*]: We're still playing hide-and-seek!

BABY DOLL [*excitedly, almost giggling*]: How long you guess we gonna be up this tree?

114

SILVA: I don't care. I'm *comfortable*—Are you?

[*Her answer is a sigh. He cracks a nut in his mouth and divides it with her. She giggles and whispers: "Shhhh!"*]

ARCHIE [*raving, sobbing, stumbling*]: Baby, my baby, oh, Baby Doll, my baby. . . .

[*Silence.*]

HEY! WOP! YELLOWBELLY! WHERE ARE YUH?

[*Aunt Rose Comfort comes forlornly out on the porch, weighed down by her ancient suitcase, roped together.*]

AUNT ROSE [*fearfully, her hair blown wild by the wind*]: Baby Doll, honey? Honey? Baby Doll, honey?

ARCHIE [*in back yard*]: I SEE YOU! COME OUT OF THERE, YOU YELLOWBELLY WOP, YOU!

[*Shotgun blasts away behind house. Aunt Rose Comfort on front porch utters a low cry and drops her suitcase. Backs against wall, hand to chest.*]

[*Fade in police siren approaching down Tiger Tail Road.*]

BABY DOLL [*nestling in Vacarro's arms in tree*]: I feel sorry for poor old Aunt Rose Comfort. She doesn't know where to go or what to do. . . .

[*The moon comes briefly out and shines on their crouched figures in the fork of the tree.*]

SILVA [*gently*]: Does anyone know where to go, or what to do?

115

114] THE YARD. ANOTHER ANGLE. POLICE CAR STOPPING BEFORE THE HOUSE AND MEN JUMPING OUT.

Shot of Meighan staggering and sobbing among the litter of uncollected garbage.

ARCHIE: Baby Doll, my baby! Yellow son of a—

115] THE YARD. ANOTHER ANGLE. SHOT OF AUNT ROSE COMFORT RETREATING INTO SHADOW AS POLICE COME AROUND THE HOUSE SUPPORTING ARCHIE LEE'S LIMP FIGURE. SHOT OF COUPLE IN TREE AS MOON GOES BACK OF CLOUDS.

Stillness. Dark. Aunt Rose Comfort begins to sing a hymn: "Rock of Ages."

AUNT ROSE: "Rock of ages, cleft for me,
Let me hide myself in Thee!"

[*Vacarro drops out of tree and stands with arms lifted for Baby Doll.*]

THE END

TIGER TAIL

The revised version of *Tiger Tail* which provides the text for this edition was produced at the Hippodrome Theatre Workshop, Inc., Gainesville, Florida, from November 2 to December 1, 1979. It was directed by Marshall New; the stage manager was Rusty Salling. Set design was by Carlos F. Asse, lighting design by Kerry McKenney, and costume design by Lisa Martin. The soundtrack was created by Peter Theoktisto; additional music for "Ruby's Song" was by Malcolm Gets. The cast, in order of appearance, was as follows:

IDEAL PAY AS YOU GO PLAN	Jerry Mason
FURNITURE CO. MOVERS	Michael Stevens
	Michael Stott
AUNT ROSE COMFORT McCORKLE	Dana Moser
BABY DOLL MEIGHAN	Jennifer Pritchett
TWO BITS	Amar Long
RUBY LIGHTFOOT	Joy Aaron
ARCHIE LEE MEIGHAN	Michael Doyle
OLD FUSSY	Rhonda
ROCK	Garland Meyer
SILVA VACARRO	Jon Schwartz
MILL HANDS	Jerry Mason
	Michael Stevens
	Michael Stott
SHERIFF COGLAN	Jerry Mason
DEPUTY TUFTS	Michael Stevens

ACT ONE

SCENE ONE

||||||||||||||||||||||||||||||||||||||||||||||||||||||||||||||||||||||||||||||||||||||||||||||||||||||||||||||||||||

Late summer. The action of the play takes place in and around the house of Archie Lee Meighan and his wife, Baby Doll, in Tiger Tail, Mississippi. The yard surrounding the crumbling old mansion is littered with garbage and the open-top remains of an old Pierce Arrow car. In the center of the set are a platform and frame, suggesting the porch.

As the audience enters the theatre, the men from the Ideal Pay As You Go Plan Furniture Company are removing what furniture remains in the house. By the time the audience is seated, all of the furniture is gone except for the crib in which Baby Doll sleeps. Litter surrounds the crib: a rocking horse, old movie magazines, candy wrappers, a pair of pink bedroom slippers, and a broken down old radio.

When the audience is seated, and the moving men have removed all of the furniture, the house lights in the theatre dim out. In the dark we hear someone dialing the telephone. A tight spot hits Baby Doll on the phone, her packed bags beside her.

||||||||||||||||||||||||||||||||||||||||||||||||||||||||||||||||||||||||||||||||||||||||||||||||||||||||||||||||||||

BABY DOLL: Kotton King Hotel? This is Mrs. Meighan, I want to reserve a room for tomorrow mornin' and I want to register under my maiden name, which is Baby Doll McCorkle. Actually, my marriage is in name only, because of an agreement Archie Lee made with my Daddy that when I was twenty years old Archie and me could be man and wife in more than just name only, well, I won't be twenty till November the seventh which is the day after tomorrow! Now, the Ideal Pay As You Go Plan Furniture Company has removed all five complete sets of furniture and I don't want to sit in the same house with a man

119

that would make me live in a house without no furniture. My daddy would turn over in his grave if he knew, he'd turn in his grave. My daddy is T. C. McCorkle who died last summer when I got married and he is a very close personal friend of the manager of the Kotton King Hotel—you know—what's his name . . .

[*Explosion and fire at the Syndicate Plantation!*

[*Aunt Rose Comfort screams. The purple night is illuminated by the garish glow of light from a huge nearby conflagration. As Baby Doll rushes out onto the porch, Ruby Lightfoot enters from the wings with Two Bits, a small boy, carrying a gallon jug of Ruby's personally distilled liquor. She is a splendid apparition, her glossy black hair, coarse as a horse's mane, piled high upon her handsome angular head. Her tight-fitting dress is of a shimmering material that catches the fiery reflections in the yard.*]

AUNT ROSE [*wildly*]: *Baby Do-oll!* Baby Doll, Baby Doll!

[*Hounds are howling, birds screeching, all the wild life about Tiger Tail Bayou except possibly the crocodiles, if any, are sounding off in alarm. Baby Doll descends cautiously into the crazily flickering yard.*]

AUNT ROSE [*screaming above the noise from porch*]: Explosion and fire at the Syndicate Plantation! Stay back, stay back, honey, you're in your nightie, folks can see right through it!

BABY DOLL: What folks, where?

AUNT ROSE: Somebody's in the yard.

RUBY: Just me, Ruby Lightfoot. I got a call while ago from Archie Lee sayin' his credit was about to be restored all through

Tiger Tail County and now I see why plain as day. Two Bits, set this jug on the po'ch, an' let's go see the show!

[*The small boy, Two Bits, runs up to the porch with the jug. He and Ruby rush off: motor heard starting, offstage.*]

AUNT ROSE: Oh, Baby Doll, that woman's delivered a jug of moonshine for Archie Lee and set it right on the porch.

BABY DOLL: Wha's Archie Lee?

AUNT ROSE: He drove off in the Chevy about ha'f an hour ago.

BABY DOLL: And ain't come back? And left us stranded here to watch the fire from this distance?

AUNT ROSE: I don't want to be closer!

[*Sound of cars and voices shouting as other residents of the community get into their cars and race off to witness the conflagration.*

[*Baby Doll bursts into childish sobs. Gradually the noise in the immediate vicinity subsides so that Baby Doll's complaints can be heard above it.*]

BABY DOLL: I'm through with that fat ole son of bitch fo' good!

AUNT ROSE: Now don't use langwidge like that.

BABY DOLL: A man that would leave me to live in a house without a stick of furniture in it except th' crib that I have to go to bed in! Well, I'll tell you something, Aunt Rose, he ain't gonna find me here when he comes back in the Chevy, no

Ma'am, I'll be downtown, checked into the Kotton King Hotel. I'm gittin' into my clo'se right now an' callin' me a Yella cab.

AUNT ROSE: Honey, you'd have to pay the hotel for a room there.

BABY DOLL: I will git me a job. The manager of the Kotton King carried my daddy's coffin, he'll give me work.

AUNT ROSE: What sort of work, Baby Doll?

BABY DOLL: I could—I could curl hair in a beauty parlor or polish nails in a barbershop—or I could be hostess at the Kotton King tea-room, just smile and pass out menus to customers coming in. There's plenty of decent employment I could find. I could be a cashier!

AUNT ROSE: Honey, you can't count change.

BABY DOLL: Whe' is my white kid purse? Oh, shoot, I left my white kid purse in the Chevy he's gone off in so I couldn't pay cab-fare downtown!

AUNT ROSE: Well, the fire's dyin' down, Archie Lee oughta be back befo' long.

BABY DOLL: He won't find me waitin' here for him when he hauls his ole ass back.

AUNT ROSE: Now stop that common talk. You just set on the swing and—keep you'self cool. Awful hot.

BABY DOLL: A Co-Cola sure would be refreshin'. [*Drops, theatrically exhausted, onto porch steps.*] Wouldja get me one outa the ice-box? Please?

122

AUNT ROSE: Honey, you had the last bottle of coke 'fore the fire broke out.

BABY DOLL: Well! —I got to have me another an' I know where to git one, too!

AUNT ROSE: Now, you can exist without another cola till Archie Lee takes you downtown fo' one.

BABY DOLL: In your opinion, not mine! I know where to get me a coke without Archie Lee and it ain't downtown.

AUNT ROSE: No place I know of, Precious.

BABY DOLL: Ruby Lightfoot has colas an' that's where I'll git me one by myself, on foot!

AUNT ROSE: Lawd, lawd, no! You at a good-time house? Unescorted?

BABY DOLL: Don't worry, Aunt Rose. Archie Lee gimme this pistol in the—

[*She rushes inside: sound of drawer slamming.*]

AUNT ROSE: No, no, no! Not in your condition, it might go off accidental!

BABY DOLL [*emerging from house*]: Don't you worry, I'll be right back!

AUNT ROSE: Wait here, I'll go with you, soon as I get my hat on! I'll go in fo' it, you stay out—outside— A woman my age is—whew!—less likely to be molested.

[*Baby Doll has already run down the road. Gun shot. Both women scream. In a few moments she runs back, gasping with horror.*]

123

AUNT ROSE [*continuing, hand to her chest*]: Baby Doll! What's happened? What're you shootin' at?!

BABY DOLL [*wild-eyed, aghast*]: A man!

AUNT ROSE: A man?

BABY DOLL: Jumped outa the bushes and stood right square in the road and he—he SHOWED himself to me, third time this month! I would of shot him daid if he'd moved at me! I scaired him silly with my pistol!

AUNT ROSE: Set down, now, honey, breathe quiet. You could a just imagined it, out of—excitement.

BABY DOLL: Plain as day I seen it in the full moon on the road! A man! I'm gonna report it to the Sheriff. You phone him!

AUNT ROSE: He would only laugh at an old woman like me.

BABY DOLL: I'll phone him m'self soon as I catch my breath.

AUNT ROSE: Honey, it would get in the paper again and you don't want that. I think maybe I got some paregoric to calm your nerves—yes, I'll fetch it right now.

[*Starting back in, she sways dizzily, clutching the door handle for support.*]

BABY DOLL: Aunt Rose! Are you all right?

AUNT ROSE: It's just been too much all at once, this experience you say happened—the fire, all that excitement— give me a dizzy spell.

BABY DOLL: Then you go right in to bed.

[*Baby Doll supports the old woman inside: the hall is lighted dimly.*]

AUNT ROSE: Child, child, be careful! I'm terrified of the future. Don't know what it holds—except death. —Promise me you'll give me a Christian burial, child, and when I'm gone, you won't disappoint my brother, bless his—

[*Their voices fade out. A moment later Baby Doll returns to the porch with paregoric and teaspoon: she leans against the screen door and pours it somewhat inaccurately into the spoon, tastes it. Baby Doll sits in swing, pouting . . . waiting. Archie Lee's car is heard turning into the drive. Archie scuttles on stage carrying an empty gallon can of coal oil and pitches it under the corner of the front porch. He walkes downstage to peer at the dim glow from the Syndicate blaze. He turns to face the porch as a dog barks at him in the distance.*]

ARCHIE: What are you doin' out here this time a-the night? Dressed like that?

BABY DOLL: I ain't talkin' to you . . .

ARCHIE: I said, what are you doing out here?

BABY DOLL: Because in the first place, I didn't have the money to pay for a hotel room, because you don't gimme any money, because you don't have any money ever since Syndicate started ginnin' all the cotton around here, and secondly, even if I had the money I couldn't have had no way of getting there because you went off in the Chevy, and left me no way of getting there or anywhere, including to the Syndicate fire which I wanted to see just like everyone else in Tiger Tail Bayou . . .

ARCHIE: What fire you talking about?

125

BABY DOLL: What fire am I talking about?

ARCHIE: I don't know about no fire.

BABY DOLL: You must be crazy or think I'm crazy. You mean to tell me you don't know the cotton gin burned down at the Syndicate Plantation right after you left the house.

ARCHIE [*seizing her arm*]: Hush up. I never left this house.

BABY DOLL: Ow!! You certainly did leave this house. OW!!

ARCHIE: Look here!! Listen to what I tell you. I never left this house.

BABY DOLL: You certainly did and left me here without a coke on the place. [*He seizes her wrist roughly.*] OWWW! Cut it out! I told you at supper I had a headache comin' on and we was runnin' out dopes, an' you said, "Yeah, git into your things an' we'll drive in town for some." But, I cain't find my white kid purse. Then I membered I left it on th' front seat of th' Chevy. An' when I come out here t' get it. Where was you? Gone off, without a word. And do you know what happened—the awful experience I had? On the road fo' Ruby Lightfoot's?

ARCHIE: Ruby's? Not possible, don't believe it!

BABY DOLL: Me desperate for a dope an' without no transportation?! On that very road . . . a man jumped outa the bushes on the road and, and—he showed himself to me!

ARCHIE: You recognize this man? Identify this man an' I'll blow his degen'rate haid off with my shotgun!

BABY DOLL: Recognized nothin' but what he done! Screamed and run back to the house! This house which ain't even fit to live

126

in! What kinda man would make me live in a house with no furniture.

ARCHIE: Aw, hell. . . . Honey, the old furniture just needs to be spread out a little . . .

BABY DOLL: My daddy would turn in his grave if he knew, he'd turn in his grave.

ARCHIE: Baby Doll, if your daddy turned in his grave as often as you say he'd turn in his grave, that old man would plow up the graveyard.

BABY DOLL: God, oh, God, what a night! First the big explosion an' fire! Then that shockin' experience on the road—feel my heart!

[*Taking this literally, he extends a hand toward her bosom and she slaps it away.*]

—Take my word! It's poundin' like a hammer!

ARCHIE [*sharply*]: Shut up!

[*He pushes her head roughly.*]

BABY DOLL: Archie! What did you do that fo'?

ARCHIE: I don't like how you holler! Holler everything you say!

BABY DOLL: What's the matter with you?

ARCHIE: Nothing's the matter with me.

BABY DOLL: WELL, WHY DID YOU GO OFF??

127

ARCHIE: I didn' go off!

BABY DOLL: You certainly did go off! Try an' tell me that you never went off when I just now seen an' heard you drivin' back in the Chevy? What uh you take me faw? No sense a-tall?

ARCHIE: If you got sense keep your big mouth shut!

BABY DOLL: Don't talk to me like that!

ARCHIE: Get on inside.

BABY DOLL: I won't. Selfish an' inconsiderate, that's what you are! I told you at supper. There's not a bottle of Co-Cola left on th' place. You said, Okay, right after supper we'll drive on over to the White Star Drugstore an' lay in a good supply. When I come out of th' house—

ARCHIE [*standing in front of her and gripping her neck with both hands*]: Look here! Listen to what I tell you!

BABY DOLL: HEY!! OWW!! Cut it out!!

ARCHIE: Listen to what I tell you. I went up to bed with my bottle after supper—

BABY DOLL: What bed! OW!

ARCHIE: And passed out dead to the world. You got that in your head?? Will you remember that now?

BABY DOLL: Let go!

ARCHIE: What did I do after supper?

128

BABY DOLL: You know what you did. You jumped in the Chevy an' disappeared after supper and didn't get back till just—OWWWWWWW!! Will you quit . . .

ARCHIE: I'm trying to wake you up. You're asleep, you're dreaming! What did I do after supper?

BABY DOLL: I don't know. OW! Went to bed! Leggo! Went to bed. Leggo! Leggo!

ARCHIE: That's right. Make sure you remember. I went to bed after supper and didn't wake up until I heard the fire whistle blow and I was too drunk to git up and drive the car. Now, go on inside and go to bed.

BABY DOLL: Go to what bed? I ain't got no bed to go to!

ARCHIE: You will tomorrow. The furniture is coming back tomorrow.

[*Baby Doll whimpers.*]

Did I hurt my little baby's arm?

BABY DOLL: Yais.

ARCHIE: Where I hurt little baby's arm?

BABY DOLL: Here . . .

ARCHIE [*putting a big wet kiss on her arm*]: Feel better?

BABY DOLL: No . . .

ARCHIE [*another kiss—this travelling up her arm*]: Oh, now, Baby Doll! My sweet baby doll. My sweet little baby doll.

129

BABY DOLL [*sleepily*]: You hurt . . . MMMmmmmmmm-mmm! Hurt.

ARCHIE: Hurt?

BABY DOLL: Mmmm!

ARCHIE: Kiss?

BABY DOLL: MMMMMMMMMMMM.

ARCHIE: Baby sleepy?

BABY DOLL: Mmmmmmmmmm.

ARCHIE: Kiss good . . . ?

BABY DOLL: Mmmmmmmmm . . .

ARCHIE: Make little room . . . good . . .

BABY DOLL: Too hot.

ARCHIE: Make a little room, go on . . .

BABY DOLL: Mmmmm.

ARCHIE: Whose baby? Big sweet . . . whose baby?

BABY DOLL: You hurt me. . . . Mmmmmmm . . .

ARCHIE: Kiss . . .

[*He lifts her wrist to his lips and makes a gobbling sound. We get an idea of what their courtship—such as it was—was like. Also how*

130

passionately he craves her, willing to take her under any conditions, including fast asleep.]

BABY DOLL: Stop it. . . . Silly. . . . Mmmmmm . . .

ARCHIE: What would I do if you was a big piece of cake?

BABY DOLL: Silly.

ARCHIE: Gobble! Gobble!

BABY DOLL: Oh you . . .

ARCHIE: What would I do if you was angel food cake? Big white piece with lots of nice thick icin'?

BABY DOLL [*giggling now, in spite of herself, also sleepy*]: Quit.

ARCHIE [*as close as he's ever been to having her*]: Gobble! Gobble! Gobble!

BABY DOLL: Archie!

ARCHIE: Hmmmmmmmmm . . .

[*He's working on her arm.*]

Skrunch, gobble, ghrumpt . . . etc.

BABY DOLL: YOU tickle . . .

ARCHIE: Answer little question . . .

BABY DOLL: What?

ARCHIE [*into her arm*]: Where I been since supper?

131

BABY DOLL: Off in the Chevy—

[*Instantly he seizes her wrist again. She shrieks. The romance is over.*]

ARCHIE: Where I been since supper?

BABY DOLL: Upstairs . . . Upstairs!

ARCHIE: Doing what?

BABY DOLL: With your bottle. Archie, leggo . . .

ARCHIE: And what else . . .

BABY DOLL: Asleep. Leggo . . . asleep! ASLEEP!

ARCHIE [*letting go*]: Now you know where I been and what I been doing since supper. In case anybody asks. An' you was aw'fly surprised w'en the Syndicate fire broke out!

BABY DOLL: Okay.

ARCHIE: Now take your things into that house and go on to bed . . .

BABY DOLL: Okay!

[*She goes inside.*]

ARCHIE: Furniture's comin' back tomorrow.

BABY DOLL: O-kay!

[*She climbs stairs punctuating each step with whimpered "Okay!" She curls up in crib and sucks her thumb.*]

ARCHIE: Okay.

[*Archie Lee stands on the front porch. He listens and hears only the cicadas and nighthawk.*]

ARCHIE [*sings*]: "My baby don' care fo' rings
                    Or other expensive things—
                    My baby just cares—fo'—me!"

[*As lights begin to fade . . .*]

Nice quiet night. Real nice and quiet.

FADE OUT

SCENE TWO

The sky is the color of the satin bows on the window curtains—a translucent, innocent blue. Heat devils are shimmering over the flat Delta country and the white front of the house is like a shrill exclamation. Baby Doll dresses in the nursery; her radio is playing, "Shame, Shame, Shame" through its tinny speaker. Aunt Rose putters about the kitchen singing. Archie Lee lumbers from back of house, semi-dressed. He stops in the hall and bellows up the stairs.

ARCHIE: Will you turn that thing down!

BABY DOLL: Aw, shut-tup!

ARCHIE: I said turn that thing down!

[She turns it up and joins in singing.]

Git outta my way, Aunt Rose!

[He moves to the mirror over the sink to finish his early morning dressing—talcum, aftershave. Aunt Rose scuttles out of his way at his bark; she busies herself with repetitive table wiping, etc. Archie then creeps upstairs to peek through the door to Baby Doll's room; he slips in and eventually announces his arrival by turning down the radio.]

BABY DOLL: Archie Lee, you're a mess in them glasses that make your eyes big as a hoot-owl's, always peekin' an' peerin'.

ARCHIE: Without 'em I couldn't see you to admire you.

BABY DOLL: Too bad they don't improve your appearance as much as your sight, you fat ole thing. No, Siree, you're not exactly a young girl's dream come true! less she was havin' a nightmare—OWWWWWW!

134

[*Archie Lee has quickly come up behind her and whacks her bottom.*]

Cut that out . . .

ARCHIE: You better quit sayin "fat ole thing" about me!!!

BABY DOLL: Well, you get young and thin and I'll quit calling you a fat old thing—

ARCHIE: You goin' around like that today? For a woman of your modest nature that squawks like a hen if her *husband* dast to put his hand on her, you sure do seem to be advertising your—

BABY DOLL [*drowning him out*]: My figure has filt out a little since I bought my trousseau *AND* paid for it with m'daddy's insurance money. I got two choices, wear clo'se skintight or go naked, now which do you want me t'—

ARCHIE: Aw, now hell—

[*The phone rings downstairs. This sound is instantly followed by an outcry even higher and shriller.*]

BABY DOLL: Aunt Rose Comfort screams ever time the phone rings.

ARCHIE: What does she do a damn fool thing like that for?

[*The phone rings again. Aunt Rose Comfort screams again. The scream is followed by high breathless laughter.*]

BABY DOLL: She says a phone ringing scares her.

ARCHIE [*shouting*]: Aunt Rose Comfort, why don't you answer the phone?

135

AUNT ROSE [*coming out of the kitchen and walking toward the hall telephone, withered hand to her breast*]: I cain't catch m' breath, Archie Lee. Phone give me such a fright.

ARCHIE: *Answer* it!

AUNT ROSE [*has recovered some now and gingerly lifts the receiver*]: Hello? This is Miss Rose Comfort McCorkle speaking, but the lady of the house is Mrs. Archie Lee Meighan, who is the daughter of my brother that passed away . . .

ARCHIE: They don't wanta know that! Who in hell is it talking and what do they want?

AUNT ROSE: I'm hard of hearing. Could you speak louder please?

ARCHIE [*storming over*]: Gi'me that damn phone.

AUNT ROSE: Archie Lee, honey . . .

[*Baby Doll's radio is blaring by this time.*]

ARCHIE: . . . and turn off that goddamn radio music.

[*Baby Doll slops over to the radio, pouting all the while and turns it off.*]

AUNT ROSE: Archie Lee, honey . . .

ARCHIE: Will you shut up and git back in the kitchen and don't speak a word. And don't holler no more in this house, and don't cackle no more in it either, or by God I'll pack you up and haul you off to th' county home at Sunset.

AUNT ROSE: What did you say, Archie Lee, did you say something to me?

136

ARCHIE: Yeah, I said shoot. [*Into receiver.*] Hello? HELLO! [*He slams down the receiver.*] Damn fools've hung up!

[*Aunt Rose cackles uneasily and enters the kitchen. Suddenly, we hear another scream from her. Lights come up in the kitchen to reveal Old Fussy, the hen, slipping into the kitchen.*

[*Silva Vacarro and his partner Rock enter the yard, talking quietly to each other. Silva's a handsome, cocky young Italian. He has a way of darting glances right and left which indicates a certain watchfulness, a certain reserve. He wears whipcord breeches, laced boots, and a white undershirt. He has a Roman Catholic medallion on a chain about his neck. In his belt he carries a whip, a small riding crop.*]

ROCK [*in a hoarse whisper*]: Maybe it figures. But it sure puzzles me why you want to bring cotton to the guy that burned down your gin . . .

SILVA: You don't know the Christian proverb about how you turn the other cheek when one has been slapped . . .

ROCK: When both cheeks has been kicked, what are you gonna turn then?

SILVA: You just got to turn and keep turning. Go on back and stop the wagons. Lemme go up to his house.

[*Rock turns to go, spots the gas can in the rubble, picks it up, with a sly grin turns to Silva.*]

ROCK: Hey, his initials are stamped right here on the can.

SILVA: S. R.?

ROCK: Yeah. Sears and Roebuck!

[*Rock pitches the can which makes a loud noise. Both laugh heartily, especially Rock.*

[*Silva walks toward the house with a disgusted look on his face at the garbage in the yard. He whistles.*

[*The sound of the laughter and the can banging to the ground, Silva's whistling and walking through the rubble has Archie bounding out of the house and onto the porch.*]

ARCHIE: Don't say a word. A little bird already told me that you'd be bringing those twenty-seven wagons full of cotton straight to my door, and I want you to know that you're a very lucky fellow.

SILVA [*dryly*]: How come?

ARCHIE: I mean that I am in a position to hold back other orders and give you a priority. Well, come on in and have some coffee.

SILVA: What's your price?

ARCHIE: You remember my price. It hasn't changed.

[*Silence. There is the sense that Silva is inspecting him.*]

Hey, now looka here. Like you take shirts to a laundry. You take them Friday and you want them Saturday. That's special. You got to pay special.

SILVA: How about your equipment? Hasn't changed either?

ARCHIE: A-1 shape! Always was! You ought to remember.

SILVA: I remember you needed a new saw cylinder. You got one?

138

ARCHIE: Can't find one on the market to equal the old one yet. Come on and have a cup of coffee. We're all ready for you.

SILVA: I guess when you saw my gin burning down last night you must've suspected that you might get a good deal of business thrown your way in the morning.

ARCHIE: You want to know something?

SILVA: I'm always glad to know something when there's something to know.

[*Rock laughs wildly.*]

Go on back to the wagons. Wait for me there.

ARCHIE: I never seen that fire of yours last night! Now come on in and have some coffee. No, sir, I never seen that fire of yours last night. We hit the sack right after supper and didn't know till breakfast time this morning that your cotton gin had burned down.

[*They go up onto the porch.*]

Yes, sir, it's providential. That's the only word for it. Hey, Baby Doll!! It's downright providential. Baby Doll!! Come out here, Baby Doll!!

[*Baby Doll enters.*]

BABY DOLL: Whu-ut?

ARCHIE: You come right over here and meet Mr. Vacarro from the Syndicate Plantation.

BABY DOLL: Oh, hello. Has something gone wrong, Archie Lee?

139

ARCHIE: What do you mean, Baby Doll?

BABY DOLL: I just thought that maybe something went—

ARCHIE: What is your first name, Vacarro?

SILVA: Silva.

ARCHIE: How do you spell that?

[*Silva spells it "Capital S-I-L-V-A." Meanwhile, his eyes are on Baby Doll.*]

Oh, like every cloud has a silver lining.

BABY DOLL: What's that from? The Bible?

SILVA: No, the Mother Goose book.

BABY DOLL: Sounds foreign.

SILVA: It is, Mrs. Meighan. I'm known as the wop that runs the Syndicate Plantation.

ARCHIE: Don't call yourself names. Let other folks call you names! I'll tell you! Gold, silver, or nickel-plated, you're a mighty lucky little fellow that I can take a job of this size right now. Of course it means cancellations. Fitting you in ahead of Baugh and Pollitt, yep, and the Sheltons, but when misfortune hits your closest neighbor, you got to accommodate him first, that's the good neighbor policy, boy! I believe in the good neighbor policy, Mr. Vacarro. You do me a good turn and I'll do you a good turn. Tit for tat. Tat for tit is the policy we live on. *AUNT ROSE COMFORT!* Baby Doll, git your daddy's sister to break out a fresh pot of coffee for Mr. Vacarro.

BABY DOLL: You get her.

140

SILVA: You sound like your business is holding up pretty good.

ARCHIE: Holding up, hell, it's expanding, it's booming, almost too much to handle! You see, when you've built up a reputation over the years as the most honest, dependable type you can deal with in a particular line, why, then, it's not a question of how much trade you can git but how much you can take care of!

SILVA: That is surprisingly good news.

ARCHIE: Surprising *how?*

SILVA: I didn't think I'd noticed much activity at the Meighan gin lately.

ARCHIE: I reckon you been absorbed too much in affairs of your own to notice mine.

SILVA: Well, now I'll have more chance to notice, won't I?

[*He is looking at Baby Doll who fans herself a bit self-consciously with a movie mag. She emits an enormous yawn.*]

BABY DOLL: Excuse my yawn. We went to bed kinda late last night.

[*Silva and Archie both notice the discrepancy.*]

ARCHIE: AUNT ROSE COMFORT!

[*Archie snaps his fingers in Baby Doll's face.*]

I said git your ole maid aunt to break out some coffee! You hear!?

141

BABY DOLL: Don't snap your fingers at me like I was a house-nigger here.

ARCHIE: Ha, ha, shoot! AUNT ROSE!

[*The volume of his call makes her scream. Archie envelops Baby Doll in an unwelcome embrace then exits into the house, calling "Aunt Rose."*]

BABY DOLL [*as if she were talking of a title of great distinction*]: So. You're a wop?

SILVA: I'm a Sicilian, Mrs. Meighan. A very ancient people . . .

BABY DOLL: Sish! Sish!

SILVA: No ma'am. Siss! Sicilian.

BABY DOLL: Oh, how unusual.

[*Archie bursts back out on the porch.*]

ARCHIE: Sometimes my baby feels neglected because I got to give so much time to my work. But this baby is my own little girl, every precious ounce of her is mine, all mine. [*Uncontrollable laughter.*] Now, Baby Doll, you entertain this young fella here while I'm ginnin' out his cotton. At noon, at noon? You take him in town to the Kotton King Hotel and buy him a chicken dinner and sign my name on the check. Yeh, I'm tellin' you—

SILVA: *What?*

ARCHIE: All right. Let's get GOING! Baby, knock me a kiss!

BABY DOLL: What's the matter with you? Have you got drunk before breakfast?

ARCHIE: Hahaha.

BABY DOLL: Somebody say something funny?

ARCHIE: Offer this young fellow here to a cup of coffee. I got to get busy ginning that cotton.

[*He extends his great sweaty hand to Vacarro.*]

Glad to be able to help you out of this bad situation. It's the good neighbor policy.

SILVA: What is?

ARCHIE: You do me a great turn and I'll do you a good turn sometime in the future.

SILVA: I see.

ARCHIE: Tit for tat, tat for tit, as they say. Hahaha. Well, make yourself at home here. Baby Doll, I want you to make this gentleman comfortable in the house.

BABY DOLL: You can't make anyone comfortable in this house. Lucky if you can find a chair to sit in.

ARCHIE [*offstage*]: Alright! Let's move those wagons. We got us some cotton to gin today.

BABY DOLL [*after a slight pause*]: Want some coffee?

SILVA: No, just a cool drink of water, thank you ma'am.

BABY DOLL: The kitchen water runs warm, but if you got the energy to handle an old-fashioned pump, you can get you a real cool drink from that cistern over there . . .

SILVA: I got energy to burn.

[*Silva strides through the tall seeding grass to an old cistern with a hand pump. He looks about contemptuously as he crouches to the cistern.*]

Dump their garbage in the yard, phew! IGNORANCE and INDULGENCE and STINK!

AUNT ROSE: Sometimes water comes and sometimes it don't.

[*The water comes pouring from the rusty spout.*]

SILVA: This time it did . . .

BABY DOLL: Bring me a dipper of that nice cool well water, please.

AUNT ROSE: I don't have the strength anymore in my arm that I used to, to draw water out of that pump.

[*She approaches, smoothing her ancient apron. Vacarro is touched by her aged grace.*]

SILVA: Would you care for a drink?

AUNT ROSE: How do you do? I'm Aunt Rose Comfort McCorkle. My brother was Baby Doll's daddy, Mr. T. C. McCorkle. I've been visiting her since . . . since . . .

[*She knits her brow, unable to recall precisely when the long visit started.*]

SILVA: I hope you don't mind drinking out of a . . .

AUNT ROSE: SCUSE ME PLEASE! That ole hen, Fussy, has just gone back in my kitchen!

[*She runs crazily to the house. Baby Doll has wandered back to the cistern as if unconsciously drawn by the magnetism of the young Italian male.*]

BABY DOLL: They's such a difference in water! You wouldn't think so, but there certainly is.

[*Silva brings up more water, then strips off his shirt and empties the brimming dipper over his head.*]

I wouldn't dare to expose myself like that. I take such a terrible sunburn.

SILVA: I like the feel of a hot sun on my body.

BABY DOLL: Yes, well, it looks to me like you are natcherally .dark.

SILVA: Yep, like you are naturally white, as white as cotton.

BABY DOLL: I'm certainly not colored, nobody could accuse me of havin' colored blood in me.

SILVA: Have I been accused of that?

BABY DOLL: I reckon with such dark skin some folks that don't like foreigners might suspicion you of havin' some colored blood in you.

SILVA: You know any folks that have expressed this opinion?

145

BABY DOLL: Well, if I did, I wouldn't repeat it, I'm not a person that tattles. Anyhow you got greenish eyes and, well, I heard you tell a nigger best by the color his gums and the roots of his finger-nails.

SILVA: Would you like to examine my gums and the roots of my finger-nails?

BABY DOLL: The subject doesn't in'trest me a-tall.

SILVA: What does interest you? Particularly, Mrs. Meighan?

BABY DOLL: Oh, I like a good movie, and I like movie magazines and I—

SILVA: Does that exhaust the number of your interests?

BABY DOLL: I'm not gonna stand out here in this hot yard and give a complete list of all my interests in life.

[*She crosses to a shade tree.*]

SILVA: But if you stood in the shade and made out a complete list of those interests in your life, I suppose that Mr. Meighan would be head of the list?

BABY DOLL: That man would be at the opposite end of the list.

SILVA: I don't want to ask embarrassing questions but I don't understand why you have married this man at the opposite end of the list.

BABY DOLL: There was—special circumstances.

SILVA: Such as? —If I may ask?

146

BABY DOLL: My daddy was a sick man for a long time and everything but his insurance money had gone on doctor an' hospital expenses and, well, he and Archie Lee was Lodge Brothers. You know. Masons.

SILVA: Engaged together in the mason's trade?

BABY DOLL: In what?

SILVA: Masonry, a form of construction?

BABY DOLL: No, no, Masons is a club, it's not—constructive or nothin'.

SILVA: Oh. A social club. I see. Tennis, golfing, all that.

BABY DOLL: Drinkin' mostly, I'd say. You could never get in it, bein' foreign an' probably—Cath'lic?

SILVA: Not sure I'd want to be in it. Prejudices like that seem—narrow-minded these days.

[*He moves closer with a slightly sensual smile.*]

BABY DOLL [*flustered*]: What was I—Oh, yes, how I got married, the circumstances. Well. Archie Lee's cotton gin was doin' good business, *then*, befo' you built *yours* and put his outa business practickly.

SILVA: I hope you don't blame me for that circumstance contributing to your—disappointment in marriage.

BABY DOLL: No, no, but life has—

SILVA: Reversals of fortune in it.

BABY DOLL: That's fo' sure.

SILVA: Now he's got a gin doing business, and I've got *what?*

BABY DOLL: You're young and—you got your health anyhow. —My daddy, he wasn't real old but his health give out. Got sicker an' sicker. He only had one liver left.

SILVA: That's the usual number of livers, Mrs. Meighan.

BABY DOLL: Kidney! I meant one kidney which was also affected! So, well, Archie Lee told Daddy he knew of this New York doctor that could take a kidney out of some kind of an ape and put this ape kidney—you shouldn't of brought up this subject. I don't want to go on with it. [*Sniffles.*] Such a—awful—heat spell . . .

SILVA: But even if it is painful to continue the subject, it would be better than not to.

[*He is very close to her, now, and her agitation increases.*]

BABY DOLL: Why? Better how?

SILVA: I am sympathetic to your story and could offer you some advice.

BABY DOLL: Well, the long and short of it is, that Archie Lee offered to fly this doctor and the ape down here for this, this—

SILVA: Operation. I think I've heard of such an operation performed somewhere, but it was the kidney of a chimpanzee.

BABY DOLL: Yeah? Well, whatever. I think Archie Lee fooled Daddy so he could get hold of me in marriage. You see, Archie Lee did not bring down the doctor like he promised and I don't think he even brought down the chim—chim—

148

SILVA: Panzee?

BABY DOLL: That's my suspicion. I think he just put Daddy in the Veterans' Hospital upstate and pretended the rest.

SILVA: The rest being what, Mrs. Meighan?

BABY DOLL [*sniffling.*]: The rest being Daddy just—died there . . .

SILVA: Now let's consider this fairly, giving Mr. Meighan the benefit of some doubt. Isn't it just possible that the chimpanzee refused to sign this paper permitting the transplant?

BABY DOLL [*slow, indignant take*]: —Mr. Vacarro, I believe that you are mistaking me for a fool!

SILVA: No, no, no, I just wanted to cheer you up.

BABY DOLL: By pretending you think I don't know a chimpanzee can't read or write!

SILVA: I've seen many remarkable things in my life!

BABY DOLL: Not monkeys signin' papers, you ain't! But my Daddy did sign a paper! Under false pretenses! And he give me to Archie Lee in marriage before the doctor and the chimpanzee got down here! My daddy, he didn't want to but in the face of death—

SILVA: I know. Compromises are made—when you're influenced—by terror . . .

BABY DOLL: —I tole you this long, awful story because you said you could offer advice. What is the advice? None? You got none to offer?

SILVA: I've got advice to offer but it takes some consideration and—Hey!

[*He indicates a derelict Pierce Arrow in the yard*]

Is this limousine retired from service?

BABY DOLL: That old automobile belonged to the widow lady that owned this place till she died and they say she still haunts it now. Sometimes I like to set in the back seat and pretend I'm a young widow and my *show*fer drives me wherever I want.

SILVA: Why don't we play that game, games can be fun, get in, Madam, be seated.

[*She smiles shyly and seats herself on the rear seat. He climbs in beside her.*]

BABY DOLL [*ambiguously discomfited by his proximity*]: Why don't you set in the front seat an' play *show*-fer?

SILVA: I'd rather play your escort. You give me directions where you want to be driven and I'll give them to the *show*-fer.

BABY DOLL: Tell him to drive us along the levee to cach the breeze off the river, fast as he can drive to cool us off.

[*She fans herself rapidly, then averting her face, sneezes.*]

—'Scuse me! The air is so full of cotton lint.

[*She sniffles.*]

—You're grinning at me like I tole you a joke!

SILVA: Not grinning, just smiling because I noticed your bracelet with all of these gold bangles.

BABY DOLL: That's what's called a charm bracelet. My daddy give it to me. There's a charm for each birthday.

SILVA: How many charming birthdays have you had?

BABY DOLL: As many as I got charms hanging on this bracelet . . .

SILVA: Mind if I count them?

[*He moves in—slowly and sensuously.*]

. . . 11, 12, 13, 14, 15, 16, 17, 18, 19 . . . and . . .

BABY DOLL: That's all! I don't want another birthday charm on that bracelet.

SILVA: You wish to end your existence at the age of nineteen.

BABY DOLL: Better than—keepin' the bargain with Archie Lee. You see, we married with the agreement that he would not—that he would leave me alone—till I was twenty. And I'll be twenty tomorrow. I don't wanna be twenty . . . ever.

SILVA: Understandable. —Don't you have garbage collectors on Tiger Tail Road?

BABY DOLL: It costs a little bit extra to git them to come out here and Archie Lee Meighan claimed it was highway robbery! Refused to pay! Now the place is swarming with flies an' mosquitoes and—oh, I don't know, I almost give up sometimes.

SILVA: And did I understand you to say that you've got a bunch of unfurnished rooms in the house?

BABY DOLL: Five complete sets of furniture hauled away! By the Ideal Pay As You Go Plan Furniture Company.

151

SILVA: When did this misfortune—fall upon you?

BABY DOLL: Why yestiddy! Ain't that awful?

SILVA: Both of us had misfortunes on the same day.

BABY DOLL: Huh?

SILVA: You lost your furniture. My cotton gin burned down.

BABY DOLL [*not quite with it*]: Oh.

SILVA: Quite a coincidence!

BABY DOLL: Huh?

SILVA: I said it was a coincidence of misfortune.

BABY DOLL: Well, sure—after all, what can you do with a bunch of unfurnished rooms.

SILVA: You could play hide and seek.

BABY DOLL: Not me. I'm not the athletic type.

SILVA: I take it you've not had this place long, Mrs. Meighan.

BABY DOLL: No, we ain't had it long.

SILVA: When I arrived to take over the management of the Syndicate Plantation . . .

[*He chops at the grass with his crop.*]

this place was empty. I was told it was haunted. Then you all moved in.

152

BABY DOLL: Yes it was haunted, and that's why Archie Lee bought it for almost nothing.

[*She pauses in the sun as if dazed.*]

Sometimes I don't know where to go, what to do.

SILVA: That's not unusual. People enter this world without instruction.

BABY DOLL [*losing the thread again*]: Huh?

SILVA: I said people come into this world without instructions of where to go, what to do, so they wander a little and . . . then go away . . .

[*Now, Baby Doll gives him a quick look, almost perceptive and then . . .*]

BABY DOLL: Yah, well . . .

SILVA: And so make room for newcomers! Old goers, new comers! Back and forth, goings and comings, rush, rush . . . Drift—for a while and then . . . VANISH. Anything living! . . . Last long enough to take it serious.

BABY DOLL: And that's all . . .

[*Silence. Possibly a mutual understanding.*]

SILVA: You're a lady to respect, Mrs. Meighan.

BABY DOLL [*sadly and rather touchingly*]: Me? Oh, no—I never got past the fourth grade.

SILVA: Why'd you quit?

BABY DOLL: I had a great deal of trouble with long division . . .

SILVA: Yeah?

BABY DOLL: The teacher would tell me to go to the blackboard and work out a problem in long division and I would go to the blackboard and lean my head against it and cry and cry and—cry . . . Whew! I think the porch would be cooler. Mr. Vacarro, I can't get over your legs.

SILVA: You can't get over my legs?

BABY DOLL: I tole you . . . I'm not athletic.

SILVA: You want me to move my legs.

BABY DOLL: Yes, otherwise I can't get out of the car . . .

SILVA: Okay.

[*He raises his legs so she can get out. Which she does, and continues . . .*]

BABY DOLL: YES, I would cry and cry . . . Well . . . soon after that I left school. A girl without education is— without education . . . Whew . . . feel kind of dizzy. Hope I'm not gettin' a SUN stroke—I better sit in the shade.

[*Vacarro follows her casually into the shade of a pecan tree. Suddenly he leaps into the branches and then down with a pecan. He cracks it in his mouth and hands her the kernels . . .*]

BABY DOLL: Mr. Vacarro! I wouldn't dream! —Excuse me, but I just wouldn't dream! of eating a nut that a man had cracked in his mouth . . .

SILVA: You've got many refinements. I don't think you need to worry about your failure at long division. I mean, after all, you got through short division, and short division is all that a lady ought to cope with . . .

BABY DOLL: Well, I—ought to go in, but I get depressed when I pass through those empty rooms . . .

SILVA: All the rooms empty?

BABY DOLL: All but the nursery. And the kitchen. The stuff in those rooms was paid for . . .

SILVA: You have a child in the nursery?

BABY DOLL: Me? No. I sleep in the nursery myself. Let down the slats on the crib . . .

SILVA: Why do you sleep in the nursery?

BABY DOLL: Mr. Vacarro, that's a *personal* question. [*There is a pause.*] I ought to go in . . . but . . . you know there are places in that house which I have never been in. I mean the attic for instance. Most of the time I'm afraid to go into that house by myself. Last night when the fire broke out I sat here for hours and hours till Archie Lee got home, because I was scared to enter this old house by myself.

[*Vacarro has caught this discrepancy.*]

SILVA: It musta been kinda scary here without your husband to look after you.

BABY DOLL: I'm tellin' you! The fire lit up the whole country-side and it made big crazy shadows and we didn't have a Co-

155

Cola in the house and the heat and the mosquitoes and—I was mad at Archie Lee!

SILVA: Mad at Meighan? What about?

BABY DOLL: . . . that he went off and left me settin' here without a Coke in the place.

SILVA: Went off and left you, did he?!!

BABY DOLL: Well, he certainly did. Right after supper and when he got back, the fire'd already broke out. I got smoke in my eyes and my nose and throat. I was in such a worn-out nervous condition it made me cry. Finally I took two teaspoons of paregoric.

SILVA: Sounds like you passed a very uncomfortable night.

BABY DOLL: Sounds like? Well it was!

SILVA: So Mr. Meighan—you say—disappeared after supper.

BABY DOLL [*after a pause*]: Huh?

SILVA: You say Mr. Meighan left the house for a while after supper?

[*Something in his tone makes her aware that she has spoken indiscreetly.*]

BABY DOLL: Oh—uh—just for a moment.

SILVA: Just for a moment, huh? How long a moment?

BABY DOLL: What are you driving at, Mr. Vacarro?

156

SILVA: Driving at? Nothing.

BABY DOLL: You're looking at me so funny.

SILVA: How long a moment did he disappear for? Can you remember, Mrs. Meighan?

BABY DOLL: What difference does that make? What's it to you, anyhow?

SILVA: Why should you mind my asking?

BABY DOLL: You make this sound like I was on trial for something.

SILVA: Don't you like to pretend like you're a witness?

BABY DOLL: Witness of what, Mr. Vacarro?

SILVA: Why—for instance—say—a case of arson!

BABY DOLL: Case of—? What is—arson?

SILVA: The willful destruction of property by fire.

[*He slaps his boots sharply with the riding crop.*]

BABY DOLL: Oh!

[*She moves to the swing and nervously fingers her purse.*]

SILVA: You know, there's one thing I always notice about you ladies.

BABY DOLL: What's that?

SILVA: Whenever you get nervous, you always like to have something in your hands to hold on to—like that big white purse.

BABY DOLL: This purse?

SILVA: Yes, it gives you something to hold on to, isn't that right?

BABY DOLL: Well, I do always like to have something in my hands.

SILVA: Sure you do. You feel what a lot of uncertain things there are. Gins burn down. No one knows how or why. Volunteer fire departments don't have decent equipment. They're no protection. The afternoon sun is too hot. The trees! They're no protection! The house—it's haunted! It's no protection! Your husband! He's across the road and busy. He's no protection! The goods that dress is made of—it's light and thin—it's no protection. So what do you do, Mrs Meighan? You pick up that white kid purse. It's something to hold on to.

BABY DOLL: Now, Mr. Silva. Don't you go and be getting—any—funny ideas.

SILVA: Ideas about what?

BABY DOLL: My husband disappearing—after supper. I can explain that.

SILVA: Can you?

BABY DOLL: Sure I can.

SILVA: Good! How do you explain it?

[*He stares at her. She looks down.*]

What's the matter? Can't you collect your thoughts, Mrs. Meighan?

[*Pause.*]

Your mind's a blank on the subject?

BABY DOLL: Look here, now . . .

SILVA: You find it impossible to remember just what your husband disappeared for after supper? You can't imagine what kind of errand he went out on, can you?

BABY DOLL: No! No! I can't!

SILVA: But when he returned—let's see—the fire had just broken out at the Syndicate Plantation.

BABY DOLL: Mr. Vacarro, I don't have the slightest idea what you could be driving at.

SILVA: You're a very unsatisfactory witness, Mrs. Meighan.

BABY DOLL: I never can think when people—stare straight at me.

SILVA: Okay, I'll look away then.

[*He turns his back to her.*]

Now, does that improve your memory any? Now are you able to concentrate on the question?

BABY DOLL: Huh?

SILVA: No? You're not?

[*He grins evilly.*]

Well—should we drop the subject?

BABY DOLL: I sure do wish you would!

SILVA: Sure, there's no use crying over a burnt-down gin. And besides, like your husband says—this world is built on the principle of tit for tat.

BABY DOLL: What do you mean?

SILVA: Nothing at all specific. Mind if I . . . ?

BABY DOLL: What?

SILVA [*approaching the swing where she sits*]: You want to move over a little and make some room?

BABY DOLL [*shifting slightly*]: Is that room enough for you?

SILVA: Enough for me. How about you?

BABY DOLL: Is it strong enough to support us both?

SILVA: I hope. Let's swing a bit. You seem all tense. Motion relaxes people. It's like a cradle. A cradle relaxes a baby. They call you "Baby," don't they?

BABY DOLL: That's sort of a pet name.

SILVA: Well in the swing you can relax like a cradle . . .

BABY DOLL: Not if you swing it so high. It shakes me up.

SILVA: Well, I'll swing it low then. Are you relaxed?

BABY DOLL: I'm relaxed enough. As much as necessary.

SILVA: No, you're not. Your nerves are all tied up.

BABY DOLL: You make me nervous.

SILVA: Just swinging with you?

BABY DOLL: Not just that.

SILVA: What else then?

BABY DOLL: All them questions you asked me about the fire.

SILVA: I only inquired about your husband—about his leaving the house after supper.

BABY DOLL: Why should I have to explain why he left the house? Besides, I did. I think I explained that to you.

SILVA: You said that he left the house before the fire broke out.

BABY DOLL: What about it?

SILVA: Why did he leave the house? What was the explanation? I forgot it.

[*Baby Doll's face is beaded with sweat. To save her life she can't think, can't think at all.*]

BABY DOLL [*just to gain a moment*]: Oh. You're talking about my husband?

SILVA: That's who I'm talking about.

BABY DOLL: How should I know!!!

SILVA: You mean where he went after supper.

BABY DOLL: Yes!! How should I know where he went.

SILVA: I thought you said you explained that to me.

BABY DOLL: I did! I explained it to you!

SILVA: Well, if you don't know, how could you explain it to me?

BABY DOLL [*turning*]: There's no reason why I should explain anything to you.

SILVA: Then just relax.

[*They swing.*]

As I was saying, that was a lovely remark your husband made.

BABY DOLL: What remark did he make?

SILVA: The good neighbor policy. I see what he means by that now. There's a lot of fine cotton lint floating around in the air.

BABY DOLL: I know there is. It irritates my sinus.

SILVA: Well, you're a delicate woman.

[*Silva removes a piece of lint with his crop.*]

There now!

BABY DOLL: Thanks. Delicate? Me? Oh, no.

SILVA: Oh, yes, every bit of you is delicate. Choice. Delectable, I might say.

BABY DOLL: Huh?

SILVA [*running his finger lightly over her skin*]: You're fine fibered. And smooth. And soft.

BABY DOLL: Our conversation is certainly taking a personal turn!

SILVA: Yes! You make me think of cotton.

[*He caresses her arm another moment.*]

No! No fabric, no kind of cloth, not even satin or silk has the ab-so-lute delicacy of your skin!

BABY DOLL: Well! Should I say thanks or something?

SILVA: No, just smile, Mrs. Meighan. You have an attractive smile. Dimples!!

BABY DOLL: No . . .

SILVA: Yes, you have! Smile, Mrs. Meighan! Come on! Smile!

[*Baby Doll averts her face, smiles helplessly.*]

There now. See? You've got them!

[*Delicately, he touches one of the indentations in her cheek.*]

163

BABY DOLL: Please don't touch me. I don't like to be touched.

SILVA: Then why do you giggle?

BABY DOLL: Can't help it. You make me feel kind of hysterical, Mr. Vacarro . . . Mr. Vacarro . . .

SILVA: Yes?

BABY DOLL [*a different attack, more feminine, pleading*]: I hope you don't think that Archie Lee was mixed up in that fire. I swear to goodness he never left the front porch. I remember it perfectly now. We just set here on the swing till the fire broke out and then we drove into town.

SILVA: To celebrate!

BABY DOLL: No, no, no!

SILVA: Twenty-seven wagons full of cotton's a pretty big piece of business to fall into your lap like a gift from the gods, Mrs. Meighan.

BABY DOLL: I thought you said we would drop the subject.

SILVA: You brought it up that time.

BABY DOLL: Well, please don't try to mix me up anymore, I swear to goodness the fire had already broke out when he got back.

SILVA: That's not what you told me a moment ago.

BABY DOLL: You got me all twisted up. We went in town. The fire broke out and we didn't know about it.

SILVA: I thought you said it irritated your sinus.

BABY DOLL: Oh my God, you sure put words in my mouth. Maybe I'd jus' better make us some lemonade.

[*She starts to get up. Silva pulls her down.*]

What did you do that for?

SILVA: I don't want to be deprived of your company yet.

[*He lightly switches her legs with his crop.*]

BABY DOLL [*twisting*]: Mr. Vacarro, you're getting awfully familiar.

SILVA: Haven't you got any fun-loving spirit about you?

BABY DOLL: This isn't fun.

SILVA: Then why do you giggle?

BABY DOLL: I'm ticklish!

SILVA: Ticklish!

BABY DOLL: Yes, quit switching me, will you?

SILVA: I'm just shooing the flies off.

BABY DOLL: Leave 'em be, then, please. They don't hurt nothin'.

SILVA: I think you like to be switched.

BABY DOLL: I don't. I wish you'd quit. Qui-it!

165

SILVA: You'd like to be switched harder.

BABY DOLL: No, I wouldn't.

SILVA: That blue mark on your wrist—

BABY DOLL: What about it?

SILVA: I've got a suspicion.

BABY DOLL: Of what?

SILVA: It was twisted. By your husband.

BABY DOLL: YOU'RE CRAZY.

SILVA: Yes, it was. And you liked it.

BABY DOLL: I certainly didn't. Would you mind moving your arm?

SILVA: Don't be so skittish.

BABY DOLL: Awright. I'll get up then.

SILVA: Go on.

BABY DOLL: I feel so weak.

SILVA: Dizzy?

BABY DOLL: Fuzzy and buzzy. My head's spinnin' round. It's that swinging. . . . Is something on my arm?

SILVA: No.

BABY DOLL: Then what are you blowin' at?

SILVA: Sweat off. Let me wipe it . . .

[*He brushes her arm with his handkerchief.*]

BABY DOLL [*laughing weakly*]: No, please don't. It feels funny.

SILVA: How does it feel?

BABY DOLL: Funny! All up and down. You cut it out now. If you don't cut it out I'm going to call.

SILVA: Call who?

BABY DOLL: That . . . that nigger boy who's cuttin' the grass across the road over there.

SILVA: Go on. Call then.

BABY DOLL: Hey!

[*Her voice is faint, weak.*]

Hey, boy, boy!

SILVA: Can't you call any louder?

BABY DOLL: I feel so funny! What's the matter with me?

SILVA: You're just relaxing . . . just relaxing. So give in. Stop getting yourself all excited.

BABY DOLL: I'm not—but you . . .

SILVA: I!???

BABY DOLL: Yes. You. Suspicions. The ideas you have about my husband . . . suspicions.

SILVA: Suspicions? Such as . . .

BABY DOLL: Such as he burnt your gin down.

SILVA: Well?

BABY DOLL: He didn't.

SILVA: Didn't he?

BABY DOLL: I'm going inside. I'm going in the house.

[*She starts in.*]

SILVA [*following close behind her*]: But you're afraid of the house! Do you believe in ghosts, Mrs. Meighan? I do. I believe in the presence of evil spirits.

BABY DOLL: What evil spirits you talking about now?

SILVA: Spirits of violence—and cunning—malevolence— cruelty—treachery—destruction . . .

BABY DOLL: Them's just human characteristics.

SILVA: They're evil spirits that haunt the human heart and take possession of it, that spread from one human heart to another human heart the way a fire goes springing from leaf to leaf and branch to branch in a tree till a forest is all aflame with it—the birds take flight—the wild things are suffocated . . . everything green and beautiful is destroyed . . .

BABY DOLL: You have got fire on the brain.

SILVA: I see it as more than it seems to be on the surface. I saw it last night as an explosion of those evil spirits that haunt the human heart—I fought it! I ran into it, beating it, stamping it, shouting the curse of God at it! They dragged me out, suffocating. I was defeated! When I came to, lying on the ground—the fire had won the battle, and all around was a ring of human figures! The fire lit their faces! I looked up. And they were all illuminated! Their eyes, their teeth were SHINING! SEE! LIKE THIS!

[*He thrusts his grimacing face at her. She springs back, frightened.*]

BABY DOLL: Hey! Please! Don't do that! Don't scare me!

SILVA: The faces I saw—were grinning! Then I knew! I knew the fire was not accidental!

[*He holds her fast at the door. He twists his face into a grotesque grimace of pleasure. He holds her.*]

BABY DOLL [*weakly*]: Not accidental?

SILVA: No, it was not accidental! It was an expression, a manifestation of the human will to *destroy*.

BABY DOLL: I wouldn't—feel that way—about it . . .

SILVA: I do! I do! And so I say I believe in ghosts, in haunted places, places haunted by the people that occupy them with hearts overrun by demons of hate and destruction. I believe his place, this house is haunted. . . . What's the matter?

BABY DOLL [*now thoroughly shaken*]: I don't know . . .

169

SILVA: You're scared to enter the house, is that the trouble?

BABY DOLL [*calling*]: Aunt Rose. Aunt Rose!!

[*No answer.*]

That old woman can't hear a thing.

SILVA: There's no question about it. This place is haunted.

[*Silva moves towards her forcing her backwards to the edge of the porch until she starts to topple over.*]

BABY DOLL: No . . . no . . . please . . . I . . . I . . . OHHHH!!!

[*He reaches out and pulls her into his arms.*]

SILVA: You're trembling, Mrs. Meighan, shaking all over!

BABY DOLL: Your—hands are so—hot—I don't think I ever felt hands as hot as your hands, they're—why they're—why they're like a couple of plates—took right off—the stove!

SILVA: Burn, do they?

BABY DOLL: Yeah, they—*do*, they *burn*—me— . . . please let me go . . . why don't I fix us a—nice pitcher of—ice cold lemonade.

SILVA: The idea of lemonade is very attractive. I would be glad to help you squeeze the lemons.

[*He tightens the pressure of his embrace.*]

BABY DOLL: I know you would! I mean I—thanks, but—I can do it myself.

170

SILVA: You don't want my assistance, Mrs. Meighan?

BABY DOLL: Naw, it ain't necessary . . .

SILVA: You want me to stay on the porch?

BABY DOLL: Yeh, you stay on the porch!

SILVA: Why *shouldn't* I come inside?

BABY DOLL: No reason, just—just . . . !

[*She giggles weakly.*]

I don't think I better. I think I will go across the road to the gin. They got a water cooler . . .

SILVA: The water cooler's for colored. A lady, a white lady like you, the wife of the big white boss, would place herself in an undignified position if she went over the road to drink with the hands! They might get notions about her! Un-wholesome ideas! The sight of her soft white flesh, so smooth and abundant, might inflame their—natures.

BABY DOLL: I'm dizzy. My knees are so weak they're like water. I've got to sit down.

SILVA: Go in.

BABY DOLL: I can't.

SILVA: Why not?

BABY DOLL: You'd follow.

SILVA: Would that be so awful?

BABY DOLL: You've got a mean look in your eyes and I don't like the whip. Honest to God, he never. He didn't I swear!

SILVA: Do what?

BABY DOLL: The fire . . .

SILVA: Go on.

BABY DOLL: Please don't!

SILVA: Don't what?

BABY DOLL: Put it down. The whip, please put it down.

SILVA: What are you scared of?

BABY DOLL: You.

SILVA: Go on.

[*Aunt Rose Comfort enters the yard from stage left with a big basket of greens. Baby Doll is both relieved to see her and indignant that she had left her alone.*]

BABY DOLL: Why, Aunt Rose Comfort, I thought you was in the house, I am surprised at you, leavin' me alone here with—

AUNT ROSE: You're not alone, Baby Doll, you're with this nice young man from the Syndicate Plantation!

BABY DOLL: That's what I mean, you left me here alone with a—a foreigner, a stranger. Some one I scarcely know.

SILVA [*quickly, with great deference*]: Please let me carry that heavy basket for you, Miss Rose Comfort.

AUNT ROSE: Thank you so much, it did seem to get so heavy on the road.

SILVA: The sun increased the weight of it.

AUNT ROSE: It did seem to, ev'ry step of the way. Sometimes Archie Lee drives me to Piggly Wiggly's Groc'ry in his automobile to shop but with all this business today, thanks to you—

SILVA: Not to me, to the *fire*.

[*They are now in the kitchen. Baby Doll, disturbed, sits in the swing.*]

AUNT ROSE: Oh, Lord, no, Mr. Vacarro, I could never give thanks to the fire!

SILVA: Perhaps Mr. Meighan could, though.

AUNT ROSE: Yais, well, frankly, Archie Lee Meighan is a very practical man that thinks mostly of his own advantage, if you know what I mean.

SILVA: I do, exactly, Ma'am.

AUNT ROSE: I should not be sayin' this while under his roof.

SILVA: But without much left in the way of the refinements of living.

AUNT ROSE: Not even a bed, Mr. Vacarro. I sleep on a—

[*Her voice breaks.*]

—pile of—ole sacks.

173

[*She weeps soundlessly for a moment, lifting her apron to her face.*]

Excuse me, I'm just so—tired. You see, Archie Lee, well, he's a *tight*-fisted man an' I don't think even prosperity would change that. He gives me, today he gave me just thirty-five cents and told me to walk in town. Six miles? Each way? Under that blazing sun? Couldn't, couldn't. I will tell you a secret. After a mile I gave up. I picked these turnip greens and dandelion greens on the road—with permission, of course, and these folks also give me a slab of fatback to prepare them with for supper. I have no worldly possessions except my friends . . .

[*The phone rings. Aunt Rose Comfort screams.*]

SILVA: What's the matter, what's the matter, Miss Comfort?

AUNT ROSE: Whenever that phone rings it makes me scream—so much bad news circulating. Excuse me. I better answer.

[*She goes to the phone as Silva tosses the greens into a big pot on the unlit stove.*]

Miss Rose Comfort McCorkle speakin'. Who are you? Oh, Bessie! How nice to hear your voice! How is Precious today? Turn for the worse? —How awful! —Honey, soon as I git my supper started I will visit her at the hospital.

SILVA: Don't wait, don't worry, if there's a hospital call, I'll see everything's took care of for supper. A bachelor learns his way around a kitchen.

AUNT ROSE [*girlishly*]: You're a bachelor, Mr. Vacarro?

SILVA: Yes, still have that misfortune.

AUNT ROSE: I'm sure it will soon be—corrected. . . . Oh, goodbye, Bessie. They's many attractive unattached girls in Tiger Tail County would set their caps for you, new manager of the Syndicate Plantation.

SILVA: Even with the cotton gin burnt down?

AUNT ROSE: Even with the cotton burned up! —You have a, you have—charming—personality, Mr.—

SILVA: Call me Silva.

AUNT ROSE [*almost flirtatious*]: Silva! —I love foreign names.

SILVA: I find that a lot of the local people are prejudiced against foreigners, specially Sicilians which they call wops. It's even been said about me I'm not completely Caucasian.

AUNT ROSE: Caw—what?

SILVA: White-blooded.

AUNT ROSE: Oh, vicious tongues, ignore 'em, ignore 'em completely!

[*Fussy appears in the open kitchen door.*]

FUSSY: Sq-u-u-u-awwwwww-k . . .

AUNT ROSE: Oh! Shoo, Fussy, shoo! You pesky critter!

[*She flaps her skirt at her and chases her into the back room of kitchen.*]

—Well, I reckon I better be on my way to the hospital now.

SILVA: —Is the hospital far? For you to go on foot?

AUNT ROSE: Not too far to make it. Always make it. . . . The poor chile . . . had such a long, tiring night, Archie Lee out so late and the—fire . . .

SILVA: The fire.

AUNT ROSE: I'll be just a while.

SILVA: Oh, take your time, don't hurry.

AUNT ROSE: I know that you'll watch out for Baby Doll.

SILVA: That was my intention, Miss Rose Comfort, you can depend on that.

AUNT ROSE: Please, excuse me.

[*Aunt Rose Comfort exits to the rear of the house. Silva returns to the porch. He slams the door startling Baby Doll.*]

BABY DOLL: Aw. You here still?

SILVA: You didn't hear your Aunt's instructions to me, Mrs. Meighan?

BABY DOLL: I'm out-done with Aunt Rose Comfort. I think it was out-*ray*-jus of her to leave me here alone with a strange man here and not a word of warning. I tell you, I sure was relieved to see her come back. That's how nervous you'd made me with all those crazy suspicions about the fire. Well. Now she's back, I s'pose I better see she gits supper started. Archie Lee gets awful cross with her when she serves it late. He's anxious to get rid of her befo' she takes sick, wants me to pack her off to some other relations but they all got excuses not to take her in. Archie Lee says if she takes sick on him here, he won't pay the cost of a doctor, he says he'll let her die, he'll just burn her up and put her ashes in a Coca-Cola bottle and throw it in Tiger Tail Bayou.

SILVA: Mr. Meighan is a man without much sentiment for the old and—homeless . . .

BABY DOLL: I'd never let her leave. I need her to be around with Archie Lee tryin' to fo'ce me to have—well, you know— If that man laid a hand on me, if he tried to, Aunt Rose would proteck me from him, like she would from you if you got too familiar. Put that in your pipe and smoke it.

SILVA: Don't have a pipe, don't smoke.

[*His hand steals about her and tightens.*]

BABY DOLL: YOU STOP THAT! —AUNT ROSE! AUNT ROSE?

[*Aunt Rose comes out of the house all dressed up.*]

BABY DOLL: Aunt Rose Comfort.

[*Aunt Rose rushes past her.*]

Aunt Rose Comfort!! Where are you going?

AUNT ROSE: I have to see a sick friend at the county hospital.

BABY DOLL: You might as well shout at the moon as that old woman.

SILVA: You didn't want her to go??

BABY DOLL: She's got no business leaving me here alone.

177

SILVA: It makes you uneasy to be alone here with me.

BABY DOLL: She just pretended not to hear me! This is just awful. I'll tell you something. Aunt Rose don't go to the hospital to call on sickly friends, she just goes there to eat up their choc'late candy! She's got a passion for choc'late candy, she'll just go there and stuff herself fulla choc'late-covered-cherries. —How far down the road's she gotten? I'm gonna call her back . . .

[*She crosses unsteadily into the yard: she shades her eyes to peer down the dirt road.*]

Aunt Rose! Aunt Rose Comfort! Come back, come back, I'm— scared . . .

[*She falls sobbing into the road. Archie Lee appears—flustered, sweating. Something is wrong.*]

ARCHIE: What're you doin' down there, have you gone crazy?

BABY DOLL: I want to tell you something! You big slob.

[*This is more than the desperate, harassed Archie Lee can bear. He smacks her good and hard!*]

ARCHIE: I told you never, never, never, to talk to me like that—specially around—

[*Rock and a few mill hands come up behind Archie Lee into the scene.*]

—our guests.

BABY DOLL [*sobbing*]: You left me . . . you know what you left me with . . .

178

[*Archie's eye wanders over to Silva.*]

SILVA: How's progress, Mr. Meighan?

ARCHIE: Fine! Great!

SILVA: Personally, I can't hear the gin at all.

BABY DOLL [*full of disgust*]: Big Shot!

[*And she pulls away to the old car chassis.*]

SILVA: What's holding up?

ARCHIE: Why, nothing . . .

SILVA: Rock!

ROCK: His saw-cylinder is busted.

SILVA: It figures. I inspected your equipment, Meighan, before I put in my own, and I put up my own cotton gin because your equipment was rotten, and still is rotten. Now it's almost mid-day and if you can't move my wagons any faster . . .

ARCHIE: Now don't go into any hysterics. You Eye-talians are prone to get too excited . . .

SILVA: Never mind about we Italians! You better get yourself a new saw-cylinder and get your gin running again. And if you can't get one in Clarksdale, you better go to Tunica, and if you can't get one in Tunica, you better go on to Memphis, and if you can't get one in Memphis, keep going to St. Louis. Now get on your horse.

ARCHIE: Now listen to me, Silva—

SILVA [*snapping his whip*]: One more crack out of you, I'm going to haul across the river. I said get on your horse.

[*Meighan hesitates—but there's nothing else for him to do under the circumstances. He exits and his old Chevy is heard pulling off at breakneck speed.*]

[*Silva continues, laughing.*]

I got a saw-cylinder in our commissary. Go get it and bring Hank over to help you put it in. Get that junk heap of his running. He ain't gonna get one in Clarksdale or Tunica and if he goes on to Memphis—

[*Everyone laughs.*]

—don't wait for him.

ROCK: Right, Boss.

[*They all exit.*

[*Silva stands proudly on porch slapping his whip on the palm of his hand.*]

BABY DOLL [*whimpering*]: Archie Lee.

SILVA: You know, Mrs. Meighan, your husband sweats more than any man I know—

[*He slaps whip in a constant beat.*]

—and now I understand why!!!

[*The sound of the whip continues as the curtain falls.*]

SLOW CURTAIN

ACT TWO

SCENE ONE

As the intermission and house lights fade, we again hear the snap, snap, snap of Vacarro's whip. Lights up reveal our two actors in the same places as the close of Act I—Silva on the porch, Baby Doll cowering by the abandoned automobile. For a moment everything is frozen except the ominous whip.

Then Baby Doll desperately runs toward the front door. As she lunges past Silva, he grabs her by the arm, jerks her close, and whispers in her ear. She gasps.

BABY DOLL: What a *disgustin'* remark! I did not understand a word of it! I am going into the house and lock the door—after such a remark which I didn't understand even . . .

[*There is a pause. Then with a sudden access of energy she enters the house, slams the screen door in his face and latches it.*]

There now! You wait out here! You just wait out here!

SILVA: Yes, ma'am. I'll wait.

[*Baby Doll stumbles into the kitchen. Vacarro jerks out a pocket knife and rips a hole in the screen.*]

BABY DOLL: What's that?!

[*Silva whistles loudly as he slips his fingers through the hole and lifts the latch.*]

BABY DOLL [*noticing kettle of greens on the stove*]: Stupid old thing—forgot to light the stove.

181

[*She hears the creaking screen door . . .*]

Archie Lee! Is that you?

[*She hears a sharp, slapping sound. Whimpering under her breath she moves anxiously into another room, out of sight of the audience. Suddenly, we hear her scream—followed by the equally startled SQUAWK! of Fussy. Silva, chuckling, hides behind the stairs.*]

BABY DOLL [*creeping into the hallway*]: Mr. Vacarro? Have you gone away, Mr. Vacarro?

[*She spots the screen door ajar.*]

Ohhhh-h-h.

[*Vacarro—out of sight—gives a soft wolf-whistle.*]

Who's that? Who's in here?

[*She climbs the stairs into the nursery.*]

Hey! What's goin' on?

[*Whip slap and soft mocking laughter, barely audible.*]

Mr. Vacarro! Are you in this house?!

[*She moves about the nursery fearfully. Stops. Cocks head and listens. Nothing. She moves into next room. Vacarro slips out of hiding and crosses into the nursery. He sees the hobby horse, lashes its rump with the whip, and slips just outside the nursery door. Baby Doll reappears to see the rocking, swaying hobby horse. She is frightened now.*]

BABY DOLL: Now, YOU! Git outta my house! You got no right to come in! Where are you?

[*Silva leaps down the stairs and hides in the kitchen. She hears a low moan from the kitchen.*]

I know it's you! You're making me very nervous! Mr. Vacarro!!! Mr. Vacarro . . . Mr. Vacarro . . .

[*With each call she creeps forward a few steps until she is back in the hallway at the foot of the stairs. All of a sudden—*]

SILVA [*springing from the kitchen*]: SQUAWK! SQUAWK!

[*She screams and runs into locked screen door and back into his arms. He grabs her viciously and rips off her skirt. She retreats as a terrified little animal from a remorselessly advancing predator. He snaps the whip and laughs.*]

BABY DOLL: No! No! Go away. Go away . . .

[*She rushes into the attic, slams the door, leans against it and listens. She hears the sound of a rusty bolt being shot. She suddenly realizes the full import of her situation, gasps, and pushes at the bolted door. Terrified, she realizes she's alone with the ghosts.*]

I've . . . I've quit. Do you hear me, Mr. Vacarro? The game is over and I've quit.

[*Silence.*]

Mr. Vacarro, will you please unlock this door and go back downstairs so I can come out . . . it is dark in here! Mr. Vacarro! I have *NEVER* been up here before! [*Whimpering.*] Oh, Mr. Vacarro, Pul-lease!

SILVA [*from behind the door*]: I wouldn't dream of leaving you alone in a dark ole attic of a haunted house—no more than you'd dream of eatin' a nut a man had cracked in his mouth. Don't you realize that?

BABY DOLL [*with sudden gathering panic*]: Mr. Vacarro! I got to get out of here. Quick! Open this door!

[*Silva makes ghostly moans.*]

BABY DOLL: MR. VACARRO!

SILVA: Do I hear a ghost in there?

BABY DOLL [*genuinely*]: Scared! Unlock the door. You're scarin' me!

SILVA: Why you shouldn't be scared of me, Mrs. Meighan. Do you think I might whip you? Huh? Scared I might whip you—

[*He slaps his boots regularly with the riding crop.*]

and leave red marks on your—body, on your—creamy white silk-skin? Is that why you're scared, Mrs. Meighan?

[*She whimpers.*]

All right. Tell you what I'm gonna do. I'm gonna take my ole whip and leave you now—leave you all alone in that attic—so you won't have to be scared of me anymore.

BABY DOLL: No-o-o!!! *Pull*ease let me out!

SILVA: But I thought you were scared of me?

BABY DOLL: I am. Let me out.

SILVA: Okay. I'll let you out. All you have to do is sign this slip of paper with this pencil I'm slipping under the door. All I want is your signature on the paper . . .

BABY DOLL: What paper?

SILVA: I guess that you would call it an affadavit, legally stating that Archie Lee Meighan burned down the Syndicate Gin . . .

[*Pause.*]

Okay?

[*Pause.*]

What do you say?

BABY DOLL: Just leave the paper, leave it right out there and when I come out I'll sign it and send it to you, I'll . . .

SILVA: Mrs. Meighan, I am a Sicilian. We're an old race of people, an ancient race, and ancient races aren't trustful races by nature. I want the signed paper now. Otherwise I'll leave you in the attic of this evil house until your husband comes home . . . *if* he ever comes home. Do you hear me?

BABY DOLL: Oooh! What am I gonna do? AUNT ROSE!

SILVA: She's gone . . . she can't hear you.

[*Pause.*]

Do what I tell you!

[*Silence.*]

BABY DOLL [*whimpering, sobbing*]: O-o-o-o-oh!

SILVA: Good-bye, Mrs. Meighan.

BABY DOLL: All right, all right . . . Hurry! Hurry!

SILVA: Hurry what?

BABY DOLL: I'll do whatever you want—only hurry!!

SILVA: Here it comes.

[*She grabs it as it comes under the door.*]

BABY DOLL: I cain't see.

SILVA: Only ghosts see in the dark.

[*She scribbles her name in frantic haste and pushes it back. We hear Vacarro's sudden, wild laugh.*]

SILVA: Thank you.

[*We hear the sound of a bolt sliding free.*]

You may come out now.

BABY DOLL: Not till I hear you! Going down those stairs . . .

SILVA: Hear me? Hear my descending footsteps on the stairs . . .

[*He slides down the banister, waits for Baby Doll's frightened face to come into view, then salutes—*]

You're "Home free"! And so am I! Bye-bye!

BABY DOLL: Where are you going? Wait, please!—I want to—

[*She comes running down the stairs.*]

I want to—

[*She doesn't complete her sentence. She looks down.*]

Was *that* all you wanted . . . ?

[*He looks at her.*]

Was me to confess that Archie Lee burnt down your gin?

SILVA: What else did you imagine?

[*The windy afternoon has tossed a cloud over the sun, now declining. She isn't looking into his face. He gives a short quick laugh and kisses her roughly on the lips, holding her head with one hand and slapping her ample rump with the riding crop. She pulls away and gasps.*]

BABY DOLL: Why . . . why, Mr. Vacarro!

[*He tucks the signed paper in his back pocket for safer keeping. He advances.*]

SILVA: No more children's games, Mrs. Meighan . . .

[*She gasps and backs upstairs into the nursery and tries to slam the door.*

[*Another soft, breathless outcry as he shoves the door open: She backs into the room containing the crib on which light has been*

187

building, somewhere between profane and sacred, giving it the aspect of a pagan altar. Silva springs into the room, thrusting the door wide open. No longer capable of an outcry, nor almost of breathing, she backs into the side of the crib. Slow with confidence, Silva advances to her, removing his shirt. The light now concentrates on their faces and the sacramental crib. The girl is paralyzed, rigid. Silva rips open her blouse and grips her hands that clutch the crib, forcing them slowly up to an almost cruciform position, his body pressed to hers. No longer capable of an outcry, she draws quick, panting breaths. All is dimmed out, now, but the altar-place of the crib, a religiously rich light on it. His head sinks between her exposed breasts.]

FADE OUT

SCENE TWO

Ruby Lightfoot's song can be heard as lights come up to reveal early evening. She sings her song as Two Bits sneaks up to the porch to place Archie Lee's jug on the steps. Both are aware of what goes on inside.

The interior of the nursery is slowly illuminated to reveal Silva curled up in the crib stroking Baby Doll who sits on the floor beside the crib. Their post-coital love play is underscored by the music.

When sensuality is dramatized it is more effective with less dependence on the spoken word, and this is especially true when both performers are visually exciting.

SILVA [*caressing her casually as he would a pet cat*]: Baby Doll . . .

[*Pause as Ruby sings.*]

BABY DOLL: Don't call me that.

[*Pause as Ruby sings.*]

SILVA: That's what your husband calls you.

[*Ruby's song concludes.*]

BABY DOLL: That's mainly why I don't like it. That ole stinker treats me like a—*thing!*

SILVA: You don't like being called by a little name of endearment?

BABY DOLL: Not one that Archie Lee calls me.

SILVA: Well, there's a good many names I've heard used around here.

BABY DOLL: Such as what?

SILVA: Precious, honey-darlin', sweetie-pie—pussy pie . . .

BABY DOLL: You're makin' fun of me, now. I've lost your respect, haven't I?

SILVA [*dreamily, with deep satisfaction*]: Not a bit, you've gained it, in exchange for that slip of paper that will make it plain as day even to blind-folded justice that Archie Lee Meighan burnt down the Syndicate gin.

BABY DOLL: That's all you wanted from me?

SILVA: It's certainly not all that I got, eh, *Bambina? Bambina mia.*

BABY DOLL: Bam *what*, what's that you called me?

SILVA: *Bambina mia*'s Italian for my baby. Do you like it?

BABY DOLL: We-ell, it's . . . it's . . .

SILVA: More appropriate, now? In private?

BABY DOLL: —How'm I gonna explain these marks that you've put on me?

SILVA: Don't explain them. Just put some cold cream and some talcum on them before you go down to supper.

[*He rises and stretches sensually and crosses to a window. His sculptural torso is framed by moonlight.*]

190

—The cotton-picking moon is out and it's full. Hound dogs are baying at it. And Archie Lee is somewhere on the road from Memphis.

[*He turns toward her.*]

—Are you tired, *bambina?*

BABY DOLL: No, not a bit. I feel real relaxed. . . . Once my daddy, when my daddy was livin', he took me to this doctor in town and tole the doctor he thought I was sufferin' from—what was it? Oh, yais, pernicious anemia . . . yeah.

SILVA: A vitality crisis?

BABY DOLL: Hmmm-Mmmm. But the doctor said, "Mr. McCorkle, your daughter is at a stage in her life when she's just waitin' for somethin' to stimulate her nature."

[*Pause.*]

Daddy didn't like that.

[*Silva laughs softly.*]

SILVA: What do you think you was waiting for, *Bambina?*

[*Pause.*]

BABY DOLL: —*You* . . .

[*Juke-box music comes from Ruby Lightfoot's place in the near distance.*]

Are we gonna have more afternoons like this?

191

SILVA [*imitating her drawl*]: Wouldn' surprise me a-tall—

BABY DOLL: You didn' answer my question.

[*She crosses to him. He draws her into his arms, thrusts his pelvis against hers, grinding slowly.*]

SILVA: "Time on my hands, you in my arms,
    Nothin' but love in vi-iiew. . . ."
Isn't that how the song goes?

BABY DOLL: You still haven't answered my question.

SILVA [*standing still*]: This is a waiting country, but there's plenty of time, oh, yes, we'll have plenty of time, for making lemonade on hot afternoons, for making love and for—

[*He laughs into her hair.*]

—"Time on our hands—" Oh, I think we're going to have time, plenty of it. It will take quite a while to construct a new gin at the Syndicate Plantation and till it is constructed and in operation I will still be bringing my wagons of cotton to Archie Lee's decrepit but still functioning gin.

BABY DOLL: You are awful, I love it . . .

[*They kiss. Archie Lee's pickup is heard on the road.*]

SILVA: Listen. I suggest we prepare ourselves to receive your husband. How do you feel about that?

[*We hear Archie's pickup crash into garbage cans in the back yard.*]

BABY DOLL: —Depressed!

SILVA: No need to be.

ARCHIE [*offstage*]: BABY DOLL! BABY DOLL! Where the hell is ever'body!

SILVA [*laughing*]: This might turn into a highly inflammable night in our lives! You greet him first.

BABY DOLL: Oh . . .

SILVA: Don't worry—I'll accept his invitation to supper!

ARCHIE [*coming into view*]: BABY DO-OOLL!!!

SILVA [*before leaping out bedroom window*]: Hey! Your wrapper!

ARCHIE: Hey! Anybody living here? Anybody still living in this house?

[*Archie Lee enters the yard; he removes a pair of thick-lensed glasses to swab his face with his shirt tail, then rubs the glasses. Suspicious, angry, something violent and dangerous is growing in his heart. He mutters to himself. He hears the soft chuckle of Ruby Lightfoot.*]

ARCHIE [*with his glasses off*]: Who's that? [*He puts the glasses on.*] Aw. Ruby. What you doin' here?

RUBY: Waitin' t' be paid fo' that gallon of sorghum molasses Two Bits set on your porch las' night and tonight.

ARCHIE: You know my credit's good.

RUBY: I seen the fire. Oh, yeah.

ARCHIE [*viciously*]: *Shuddup!* —I am married to a respectable young lady so I'd be much obliged if you'd not come onto the front yard in that kind of outfit. My Baby Doll would be shocked. Now *GIT* outta here! I said GIT!

193

[*She laughs mockingly as she eludes his attempt to grab her. He snorts. He takes a long gulp of the contents of the jug. Two Bits seizes the chance to run past Archie Lee after Ruby, startling the flustered redneck. Aunt Rose Comfort is lighted in the kitchen-dining-room area. She has not yet discovered that the stove isn't burning.*]

ARCHIE [*turning into the house*]: BABY DOLL! —Thought I'd smell something cookin' for supper in here!

AUNT ROSE: Oh! It's you, Archie Lee!

ARCHIE [*entering the kitchen area*]: Who the hell else didja think it might be?

AUNT ROSE: I didn't hear you arrive. It's been such an unusual afternoon. I paid a call on a sickly friend of mine at the county hospital.

ARCHIE: Eatin' chocolates, huh?

AUNT ROSE: She was in this see-through tent to help her breathe oxygen, but while I was with her it turned itself off somehow and she . . . she . . . she. . . . Little Precious is gone, and I want you to know that they accused me of turning off the machine. There was this big fuss about it till I told who I was, that I was Miss Rose Comfort McCorkle devoted to Little Precious and jus'—

ARCHIE: Eatin' choc'lates while she kicked the bucket.

[*He notices the sound above.*]

Wha's my Baby Doll?

AUNT ROSE: I think that she's been restin'.

ARCHIE: —CHRIST!

[*He shouts up the stairs.*]

HEY!

[*He starts up the stairs. Baby Doll appears on them in her flimsy wrapper.*]

—What's the meanin' of this?

BABY DOLL: Meanin' of what?

ARCHIE: You drest that way?

BABY DOLL: I just had me a bath and when I heard you down here, I couldn't wait to see you, you know that.

ARCHIE: What's them marks on your body?

BABY DOLL: Aw, them's mosquito bites. I scratched 'em— Lemme *go!*

ARCHIE: Ain't I told you not to slop around here like that???!!

AUNT ROSE [*alarmed by the shout, appears in the door to the kitchen, crying out thin and high.*]: Almost ready, now, folks, almost ready!!

[*She rushes back into the kitchen with her frightened cackle. There is a crash of china from the kitchen.*]

ARCHIE: The breakage alone in this kitchen could ruin a well-to-do man. Whew! *Twen*-ty *sev*-en *wa*-gons *full* of *cot*-ton! *Some day's work!*

[*A dog howls. Baby Doll utters a breathless laugh.*]

What're you laughin' at, honey? Not at me I hope. I'm all wo'n out an' I want a little appreciation not—silly giggles like that!

BABY DOLL: You're not the only one's—done a big day's—work.

ARCHIE: Who else that you know of?

[*There is a pause. Baby Doll's laughter spills out again.*]

You're laughin' like you been on a goddam jag.

[*Baby Doll laughs.*]

What did you get pissed on? Roach poison or citronella? I think I make it pretty easy for you, workin' like a mule skinner.

[*Baby Doll says: "Sure* (laughs) . . . *you make it easy!" while Archie continues.*]

I've yet to see you lift a finger. Even gotten . . . too lazy t' put you' things on. Round the house ha'f naked all th' time. All you can think of is "Give me a Coca-Cola!" Well, you better look out. They got a new bureau in the guvamint files. It's called U.W.A. Stands for Useless Wimmen of America. Tha's secret plans on foot t' have 'em shot!

AUNT ROSE: Almost ready, folks, almost ready!

BABY DOLL: How about men that's destructive? Don't they have secret plans to round up men that's destructive and shoot them too?

ARCHIE: What destructive men you talkin' about?

BABY DOLL: Men that blow things up and burn things down because they're too evil and stupid to git along otherwise.

196

Because fair competition is too much for 'em. So they turn criminal. Do things like arson. Willful destruction of property by fire.

[*She steps out on the porch. Night sounds. A cool breeze tosses her damp curls. She sniffs the night air like a young horse. . . . The porch light, a milky globe patterned with dead insects, turns on directly over her head.*]

ARCHIE: Who said that to you, where'd you git that from?

BABY DOLL: Turn that porch light off, there's men on the road can see me.

ARCHIE: Who said *arson* to you? Who spoke of willful destruction of— YOU never known them words. Who SAID 'em to yuh?

BABY DOLL: Sometimes, Big Shot, you don't seem t' give me credit for much intelligence! I've been to school, in my life, and I'm a—magazine reader!

[*She shakes off his grip and starts down the porch steps.*

[*There is a group of men on Tiger Tail Road. One of them gives a wolf whistle. At once, Archie Lee charges down the steps—crying out—*]

ARCHIE: *Who gave that whistle??* Which one of you give a wolf-whistle at my wife?

[*Ruby Lightfoot announces her return with characteristic flamboyance.*]

RUBY: *Hey, there, Daddy, Ruby's back!*

197

ARCHIE: *Didn't I tellya to keep your ass—?*

RUBY [*drawing a knife*]: Don't say it! Don't gimme no mouth, I'm back for cash that you've had time to collect off that fine new client of yours. Two Bits, go make the collection off him, he knows the bill and the bill refuses to wait!

BABY DOLL: Has she come back with more liquor for Archie Lee to celebrate—?

ARCHIE [*turning to Baby Doll with his hand lifted*]: *Shut your goddam—*

BABY DOLL: His criminal action las' night?

[*Meighan slaps her viciously. Two Bits exits running in response to the violent slap.*]

RUBY: Hey, now!

BABY DOLL: That's the last time you'll lay a hand on me!

ARCHIE: I'll lay more'n a hand on you in less'n three hours. . . . You will be age twenty and I will celebrate plenty!

[*Ruby laughs and Archie whirls back to face her.*]

Now, you, moonshiner, haul your ass off my property! Back to the bayou with it!

RUBY: Moonshiner, who? Don't lay that name on me! Though, I suspects that's all you gonna be layin' tonight . . .

[*Ruby exits.*]

BABY DOLL: Small dawgs got a loud bark, specially at a full moon . . .

||||||||||||||||||||||||||||||||||||||||||||||||||||||||||||||||||||||||||||||||||||||||||||||||||||||||||||||||||

ARCHIE: That gang of men was from the Syndicate Plantation, white an' black mixed, headed for Tiger Tail Bayou with
frog-gigs and with rubber boots on! I just hope they turn
downstream an' trespass on my property! I hope they dast do!
I'll blast 'em out of the bayou with a shotgun! Nobody's gonna
insult no woman of *mine!*

BABY DOLL: You take a lot for granted when you say *mine.*
This afternoon I think maybe you didn't understand th' good
neighbor—policy.

ARCHIE: Don't understand it? Why I'm the boy that invented
it.

BABY DOLL: Huh-huh! What an—*invention!* All I can say
is—I hope you're satisfied now that you've ginned out twenty-
seven wagons full of cotton. I for one, have got no sympathy for
you, now or ever. An' the rasslin' match between us is *over* so let
me *go!*

ARCHIE: You're darn tootin' it's over. In just three hours the
terms of the agreement will be settled for good.

BABY DOLL: Don't count on it. That agreement is cancelled.
Because it takes two sides to make an agreement, like an
argument, and both sides got to live up to it completely. You
didn't live up to yours. Stuck me in a house which is haunted
and five complete sets of unpaid-for furniture was removed
from it las' night. OOHH I'm *free* from my side of that bargain.

ARCHIE: *Sharp at midnight!* We'll find out about that.

BABY DOLL: Too much has happened here lately . . .

ARCHIE: [*eying her figure, sweating, licking his chops*]:
Well . . . my credit's wide open again!

199

BABY DOLL: So is the jailhouse door wide open for you if the truth comes out.

ARCHIE: You threatnin' me with—blackmail??

BABY DOLL: Well, well, well . . . look who's drawin' some cool well water from the pump out there.

[*The full frog-gigging moon emerges from a mackerel sky, and we see Silva making his ablutions at the cistern pump with the zest and vigor of a man satisfied.*]

BABY DOLL [*with unaccustomed hilarity*]: HEIGH HO SIL-VER . . . HaHa!!

[*Archie stops dead in his tracks.*]

BABY DOLL: Give me another drink of that sweet well water, will yuh, Mistuh Vacarro? You're the first person could ever pump it. Archie Lee, Mr. Vacarro says he might not put up a new cotton gin, but let you gin cotton for him all the time now. Ain't you pleased about that? Tomorrow he plans to come with lots more cotton, and maybe another twenty-seven wagonloads. And while you're ginning it out, he'll have me entertain him, make lemonade for him. It's going to go on and on! Maybe even next fall.

SILVA [*through the water*]: Good neighbor policy in practice.

[*Having wetted himself down he now drinks from the gourd.*]

I love well water. It tastes as fresh as if it never was tasted before. Mrs. Meighan, would you care for some more?

BABY DOLL: Why thank you, yes, I would.

[*There is a grace and sweetness and softness of speech about her, unknown before . . .*)

SILVA: Cooler nights have begun.

ARCHIE [*who has been regarding the situation, with its various possibilities, and is far from content*]: How long you been on the place?

SILVA [*drawling sensuously with his eyes on the girl*]: All this unusually long hot afternoon I've imposed on your hospitality. You want some of this well water?

ARCHIE [*with a violent gesture of refusal*]: Where you been here???

SILVA: Taking a nap on your only remaining bed. The crib in the nursery with the slats let down. I had to curl up on it like a pretzel, but the fire last night deprived me of so much sleep that almost any flat surface was suitable for slumber.

[*He winks impertinently at Archie Lee, then turns to grin sweetly at Baby Doll, wiping the drippings of well water from his throat.*]

But there's something sad about it. Know what I mean?

ARCHIE: Sad about what??

SILVA: An unoccupied nursery in a house, and all the other rooms empty . . .

ARCHIE: That's no problem of yours!

SILVA: The good neighbor policy makes your problems mine—and vice versa . . .

AUNT ROSE [*violent and high and shrill*]: SUPPER! READY! CHILDREN . . .

[*She staggers back in. Now there's a pause in which all three stand tense and silent about the water pump. Baby Doll with her slow, new smile speaks up first . . .*]

BABY DOLL: You all didn't hear us called in to supper?

ARCHIE: You gonna eat here tonight?

SILVA: Mrs. Meighan asked me to stay for supper but I told her I'd better get to hear the invitation from the head of the house before I'd feel free to accept it. So. . . . What do you say?

ARCHIE [*a tense pause . . . then, with great difficulty . . .*]: Stay! . . . fo' supper.

BABY DOLL: You'll have to take potluck.

SILVA: I wouldn't be putting you out?

[*This is addressed to Baby Doll, who smiles vaguely and starts toward the house.*]

BABY DOLL: I better get into my clo'se . . .

ARCHIE: Yeah . . . hunh . . .

[*They follow her sensuous departure with their eyes till she fades into the dusk.*]

Did I understand you to say you wouldn't build a new gin but would leave your business to me?

202

SILVA: If that's agreeable to you . . .

ARCHIE [*turning from his wife's back to Silva's face*]: I don't know yet, I'll have to consider the matter. . . . Financing is involved such as—new equipment. . . . Let's go in and eat now. . . . I got a pain in my belly, I got a sort of heart-burn . . .

[*They enter the kitchen. Archie Lee's condition is almost shock. He can't quite get with the situation. He numbly figures that he'd better play it cool till the inner fog clears. But his instinct is murder. His cowardly caution focuses his malice on the old woman and the unsatisfactory supper she's prepared.*]

Hey! Hey! One more place at the table! Mr. Vacarro from the Syndicate Plantation is stayin' to supper.

AUNT ROSE: Just let me—cut some roses!

ARCHIE: Another place is all that's called for. Have you been here all day?

AUNT ROSE: What was that you say, Archie Lee?

ARCHIE: HAVE YOU BEEN IN THE HOUSE ALL AFTERNOON OR DID YOU LIGHT OUT TO THE COUNTY HOSPITAL TO EAT SOME DYING WOMAN'S CHOCOLATE CANDY???

AUNT ROSE [*gasping as if struck, then cackling . . .*]: I—I—visited! an old friend in a—coma! Like I told you!

ARCHIE: Then you wasn't here while I was—

[*He turns to Vacarro—fiercely.*]

I work like the hammer of hell! I come home to find the kitchen

TIGER TAIL

IIIIIIIIIIIIIIIIIIIIIIIIIIIIIIIIIIIIIIIIIIIIIIIIIIIIIIIIIIIIIIIIIIIIIIIIIIIIIIIIIIIIIIIIIIIIIIIIIIIIIIIIIIIIIIIIIIIIIIIIIIIIIIIIIIIIIIIII

all broken glass, my wife bad-tempered, insulting! and a supper of hog slops— Sit down, eat. I got to make a phone call.

[*He crosses somewhat uneasily to the phone, picks it up as Baby Doll descends the steps, goes past him with her face austerely averted. She is clad in a fresh silk sheath and is adjusting an earring as she enters the kitchen.*]

BABY DOLL: He's at the phone about something and if I was you, I wouldn't hang around long.

SILVA: I think I've got a pretty good little witness.

BABY DOLL: Don't count on a law court. Justice around here is as deaf and blind as that old woman.

SILVA: I find you different this evening in some way. Suddenly grown up.

BABY DOLL [*looking at him gratefully*]: I feel cool and rested, for the first time in my life. I feel that way, rested and cool.

[*A pause. We hear Archie Lee on the phone.*]

Are you staying or going???

[*They are close together by the table. Suddenly she catches her breath and flattens her body to his. The embrace is active. She reaches above her and pulls the beaded chain of the light bulb, plunging the room into darkness. We hear two things: the breath of the embracing couple and the voice of Archie Lee on the phone.*]

ARCHIE: A bunch of men from the Syndicate Plantation are out frog-giggin' on Tiger Tail Bayou and I thought we all might join the party. How about meetin' at the Brite Spot in half'n hour? With full equipment.

[*A few more indistinct words, he hangs up. The light is switched back on in the kitchen. Aunt Rose rushes in.*]

AUNT ROSE: Roses! Poems of nature . . . poems of nature . . .

ARCHIE [*entering from the hall, his agitation steadily mounting*]: Never mind poems of nature, just put food on th' table!

AUNT ROSE: If I'd only known that company was expected, I'd . . .

[*Her breathless voice expires as she scuttles about putting roses in a vase.*]

Only takes a minute.

ARCHIE: We ain't waitin' no minute. Bring out the food.

BABY DOLL: Don't pick on Aunt Rose . . .

ARCHIE [*shouting*]: Put some food on the table!!! [*Muttering.*] I'm going to have a talk with that old woman, right here tonight. She's outstayed her welcome.

SILVA [*changing the subject*]: What a pretty wrapper you're wearing tonight, Mrs. Meighan.

BABY DOLL [*coyly*]: Thank you, Mr. Vacarro.

SILVA: If you don't mind my saying it, but it's very flattering to your figure.

ARCHIE [*screaming*]: FOOD! FOOD!

SILVA: There's so many shades of blue. Which shade is that?

205

BABY DOLL: Jus' baby blue.

ARCHIE: Baby blue, my ass. FOOD!

SILVA: Your wrapper brings out the color of your eyes.

ARCHIE: FOOD! FOOD!

AUNT ROSE: Immediately! This instant!

[*She places the greens on the table. They are raw.*]

BABY DOLL: This wrapper was part of my trousseau, as a matter of fact. I got all my trousseau in Memphis at various departments where my daddy was known. Big department stores on Main Street.

ARCHIE: WHAT IS THIS STUFF???!! GRASS??!!

BABY DOLL: Greens! Don't you know greens when you see them?

ARCHIE: This stuff is greens??!!

AUNT ROSE: Archie Lee dotes on greens, don't you, Archie Lee?

ARCHIE: No, I don't!

AUNT ROSE: You don't? You . . . you don't dote on greens?

ARCHIE: I don't think I ever declared any terrible fondness for greens in your presence, Aunt Rose!

AUNT ROSE: Well, somebody did.

ARCHIE [*raving*]: Somebody did—sometime, somewhere, but that don't mean it was me!

BABY DOLL [*who is holding Silva's hand under the table*]: Sit down, Big Shot, an' eat your greens. Greens puts iron in your system.

ARCHIE: This ain't even fit for hog slops. I'm gonna have a talk with you, woman—tonight! You've outstayed your welcome.

AUNT ROSE: But I . . . I thought Archie Lee doted on greens! —All those likes an' dislikes are hard to keep straight in your head. But Archie Lee's easy to cook for. Jim's a complainer, oh, my, what a complainer Jim is, and Susie's household, they're nothing but complainers.

ARCHIE: TAKE THIS SLOP OFF TH' TABLE!!!

AUNT ROSE: I'll—cook you some—eggs Birmingham! —These greens didn' cook long enough. I played a fool trick with my stove. I forgot to light it! Ha ha! When I went out—I had my greens on the stove. I thought I'd left 'em boilin'. But when I got home I discovered that my stove wasn't lighted.

ARCHIE: Why do you say "my" stove. Why is everything "my."

BABY DOLL: Archie Lee, I believe you've been drinkin'!

ARCHIE: You keep out of this! Set down, here, Aunt Rose.

AUNT ROSE: Why don't I just light up my stove an' cook you up some eggs Birmingham. I won't have my men-folks unsatisfied with their supper. Won't have it. Won't stand for it!

SILVA: What is eggs Birmingham, Miss McCorkle?

AUNT ROSE: Why, eggs Birmingham was Baby Doll's daddy's pet dish.

SILVA: Now that doesn't answer my question.

AUNT ROSE [*as though confiding a secret*]: I'll tell you how to prepare them.

BABY DOLL: He don't care how you prepare them, Aunt Rose, jes' what they are!

AUNT ROSE: Well, honey, I can't say what they are without telling how to prepare them. You cut some bread slices and take the centers out of them. You put the bread slices in a skillet with butter. Then into each cut-out center you drop one egg and on top of the eggs you put the cut-out centers.

ARCHIE [*sarcastically*]: Do you build a fire in th' stove?

BABY DOLL: No, you forget to do that. That's why they call them eggs Birmingham, I suppose.

[*She laughs at her own wit, and Silva follows with a good laugh.*]

ARCHIE: Aunt Rose! Set down! I want to ask you a question.

[*Aunt Rose Comfort sits down slowly and stiffly, all atremble.*]

What sort of—plans have you made?

AUNT ROSE: Plans, Archie Lee? What sort of plans do you mean?

ARCHIE: Plans for the future!

208

BABY DOLL: I don't think this kind of discussion is necessary in front of company.

SILVA: Mr. Meighan, when a man is feeling uncomfortable over something, it often happens that he takes it out on some completely innocent person just because he has to make somebody suffer.

ARCHIE: You keep out of this too. I'm askin' Aunt Rose a perfectly sensible question. Now, Aunt Rose. You been here since August and that's a mighty long stay. Now, it's my honest opinion that you're in need of a rest. You been cookin' around here and cookin' around there for how long now? How long you been cookin' around people's houses?

AUNT ROSE [*barely able to speak*]: I've helped out my— relatives—folks—whenever they—*needed me to!* I was always— *invited!* Sometimes *begged* to come! When *babies* were expected or when somebody was *sick*, they called for Aunt Rose, and Aunt Rose was always—ready. . . . Nobody *ever* had to— *put-me-out!* —If you—gentlemen will excuse me from the table—I will pack my things! If I hurry I'll catch the nine o'clock bus to—

[*She can't think "where to."*]

SILVA [*rising*]: Miss Rose Comfort. Wait. I'll drive you home.

AUNT ROSE: —I don't!—have nowhere to!—go . . .

SILVA [*crossing to her*]: Yes, you do. I need someone to cook for me at my place. I'm tired of my own cooking and I am anxious to try those eggs Birmingham you mentioned. Is it a deal?

AUNT ROSE: —Why, I—

BABY DOLL: Sure it's a deal. Mr. Vacarro will be good to you, Aunt Rose Comfort, and he will even *pay* you, and maybe— well y'never can tell about things in the future . . .

AUNT ROSE: *I'll run pack my things!*

[*She resumes a reedy hymn in a breathless cracked voice as she goes upstairs.*]

ARCHIE: Anything else around here you wanta take with yuh, Vacarro?

[*Silva looks around coolly as if considering the question. Baby Doll utters a high, childish giggle.*]

Well, *is* they? Anything else around here you wanta take away with yuh?

BABY DOLL [*raising gaily*]: Why, yaiss, Archie Lee. Mr. Vacarro noticed the house was overloaded with furniture and he would like us to loan him five complete sets of it to—

ARCHIE [*seizing the jug of liquor*]: YOU SHUDDUP! I will git to you later.

BABY DOLL: If you ever git to me it sure is going to be *later*, ha ha, much later, ha ha.

[*Baby Doll crosses to the kitchen sink, arranging her kiss-me-quicks in the soap-splashed mirror, also regarding the two men behind her with bland satisfaction. She hums away. Archie Lee stands by the table, breathing heavy as a walrus in labor. He looks from one to the other. Silva coolly picks up a big kitchen knife and lops off a hunk of bread, then tosses the kitchen knife out of Archie Lee's reach and dips the bread in the pot of greens.*]

SILVA: Colored folks call this pot liquor.

BABY DOLL: I love pot liquor.

SILVA: Me, too.

BABY DOLL [*dreamily*]: —Crazy 'bout pot liquor . . .

[*She turns around and rests her hips against sink. Archie Lee's breathing is loud as a cotton gin, his face fiery. He takes swallow after swallow from the jug. Vacarro devours the bread.*]

SILVA: Mm-UMMM!

BABY DOLL: Good?

SILVA: *Yes! —Good!*

BABY DOLL: —*That's* good . . .

[*Old Fussy makes a slow stately entrance, pushing the door open wider with her fat hips and squawking peevishly at this slight inconvenience. Archie Lee wheels about violently and hurls something at her. She flaps and squawks back out.*

[*Baby Doll giggles.*]

Law! Ole Fussy mighty near made it that time! Why, that old hen was comin' in like she had been invited t' supper.

[*Her giggly voice expires as Archie Lee wheels back around and bellows. Archie Lee explodes volcanically. His violence should give him a Dostoevskian stature. It builds steadily through the scene as a virtual lunacy possesses him with the realization of his hopeless position.*]

211

ARCHIE: OH HO HO HO HO! Now you all listen to me! Quit giving looks back and forth an' listen to me! Y'think I'm deaf, dumb an' blind or somethin', do yuh? You're *mistook*, Oh, brother, but you're much, much—*mistook!* Ohhhhh, I knooooow! —I guess I look like a—I guess I look like a—

[*Panting, puffing pause; he reels a little, clutching a chair back.*]

BABY DOLL [*with an insolently childish lisp*]: What d'you guess you look like, Archie Lee? Yo' was about t' tell us an' then yuh quit fo' some—

ARCHIE: *Yeah, yeah, yeah!* Some little innocent Baby Doll of a wife not yet ready fo' marriage, oh no, not yet ready for marriage but plenty ready t'— Oh, I see how it's funny, I can see how it's funny, I see the funny side of it. *Oh ho ho ho ho!* Yes it sure is comic, comic as hell! But there's one little teeny-eensy little—thing that you—*overlooked!* I! Got *position!* Yeah, yeah, *I* got *position!* Here in this county. Where I was bo'n an' brought up! I hold a respectable position, lifelong!—member of— Wait! Wait! Baby Doll . . .

[*Baby Doll has started to cross past him; he seizes her wrist. Vacarro stirs and tenses slightly but doesn't rise or change his cool smile.*]

ARCHIE: On my side're friends, long standin' *bus'ness* associates, an' *social!* See what I mean? You ain't got that advantage, have yuh, mister? Huh, mister? Ain't you a dago, or something, excuse me, I mean Eyetalian or something, here in Tiger Tail County?

SILVA: Meighan, I'm not a doctor, but I was a medical corpsman in the Navy and you've got a very unhealthy looking flush on your face right now—almost as purple as a—

[*He was going to say "baboon's ass."*]

ARCHIE [*bellowing out*]: ALL I GOT TO DO IS GIT ON THAT PHONE IN THE HALL!

SILVA: And call an ambulance from the county hospital?

ARCHIE: Hell, I don't even need t' make a phone call! I can handle this situation *m'self!*—with legal protection that no one could—

SILVA [*still coolly*]: What situation do you mean, Meighan?

ARCHIE: Situation which I come home to find here under my roof! Oh, I'm not such a marble-missing old fool! I couldn't size it up! —I sized it up the moment I seen you was still on this place and *her!*—with that *sly smile on her!*

[*He takes a great swallow of liquor from the fresh jug.*]

And *you* with *yours* on *you!* I know how to wipe off both of those sly—!

[*He crosses to the closet door. Baby Doll utters a gasp and signals to Vacarro to watch out. Vacarro rises calmly.*]

SILVA: Meighan?

[*He speaks coolly, almost with a note of sympathy.*]

You know, and *I* know, and I *know* that you *know* that I *know!* — That you set fire to my cotton gin last night. You burnt down the Syndicate Gin and I got a confession and a witness whose testimony will hold up even in the law courts of Tiger Tail County! —That's all I come here for and that's all I got . . . whatever else you suspect—well!—you're mistaken. . . . Isn't that so, Mrs. Meighan? Isn't your husband mistaken in thinking that I got anything out of this place but *proof*, which was the purpose of my all-afternoon call?

[*She looks at him, angry, hurt. Archie Lee wheels about, panting.*]

Yes, I'm foreign but I'm not revengeful, Meighan, at least not more than is rightful.

[*He smiles sweetly.*]

—I think we got a workable good neighbor policy between us. It might work out, anyhow I think it deserves a try. Now as to the other side of the situation, which I don't have to mention. Well, all I can say is, a certain attraction—exists! Mutually, I believe! I took a nap in the nursery crib and I have a faint recollection of being sung to by someone—a lullaby song that was—sweet . . .

[*His voice is low, caressing.*]

—and the touch of—cool fingers.

ARCHIE: Y'think I'm gonna put up with this—?

SILVA: Situation? You went to a whole lot of risk an' trouble to get my business back. Now don't you want it? It's up to you, Meighan, it's—

ARCHIE: COOL! Yeah, cool, very cool!

SILVA: The heat of the fire's died down . . .

ARCHIE: UH HUH! YOU'VE FIXED YOUR WAGON! WITH THIS SMART TALK, YOU JUST NOW FIXED YOUR WAGON! I'M GONNA MAKE A PHONE CALL THAT'LL WIPE THE GRIN OFF YOUR GREASY WOP FACE FOR GOOD!

[*He charges into the hall and seizes the phone.*]

SILVA [*crossing to Baby Doll at the kitchen sink*]: Is my wop face greasy, Mrs. Meighan?

[*She remains at the mirror but her childish smile fades. Her face goes vacant and blind: she suddenly tilts her head back against the bare throat of the man standing behind her. Her eyes are clenched shut. . . . His eyelids flutter as his body presses against all the mindless virgin softness of her abundant young flesh. We can't see their hands, but hers are stretched behind her, his before him.*]

ARCHIE [*in the hall, bellowing like a steer*]: I WANT SPOT, MIZZ HOPKINS, WHE' IS SPOT!?

BABY DOLL [*to Vacarro*]: I think you better go 'way . . .

SILVA: I'm just waiting to take you girls away with me . . .

BABY DOLL [*softly as if in a dream*]: Yeah. I'm goin' too. I'll check in at the Kotton King Hotel and— now I better go pack . . .

[*She releases herself regretfully from the embrace and crosses into the hall.*]

[*Silva looks after her. As she passes Archie Lee she utters a sharp outcry as Archie Lee strikes at her.*]

BABY DOLL: You ole son of a bitch, you're gonna be sorry for ev'ry time you laid your ugly ole hands on me, you stinking stinker, *stinkerrrrrr!*

[*He has drawn back his hand to smack her again, but quick as lightning she snatches his thick-lensed glasses from his prominent nose and tosses them over her head.*]

BABY DOLL: There now! How's your eye-sight?

ARCHIE: Bitch! Bitch! Gimme back my glasses!

BABY DOLL: Colleck 'em in hell!

[*Archie Lee stumbles dizzily about when he hears the screen door slamming on Silva's exit. He starts crashing into chairs, the table, etc. Baby Doll watches with silent laughter from the hall. Archie has trouble locating the kitchen closet. While he is fumbling for it, Baby Doll dashes past the closet to the phone area and snatches the phone from the bare floor.*]

BABY DOLL [*in a tense whisper*]: Operator, git me the police chief of Tiger Tail, yais, the chief, not just the police. Quick, a crazy man's in the house tryin' t' grab me! Aw! Chief! This is Baby Doll McCorkle, the ex-Mrs. Meighan out in the haunted house on Tiger Tail Road! You heah that commotion? That's my ex-husband, Archie Lee Meighan, tryin' to git his shotgun out of the closet. Oh my God, he's got the gun-closet open, he's—

[*Archie Lee seizes a broom then discovers his mistake with a howl of rage. He crashes against the wall. His nose is bloodied, but now he has his shotgun. Vacarro gives Baby Doll a soft whistle as she darts into the yard. He stands by the pecan tree, clutches a lower branch and swings up into a wide fork of the tree then leans over to lift Baby Doll up beside him. The fork is almost free of foliage so they are clearly visible.*]

SILVA: Climb higher so Meighan can't see us!

BABY DOLL [*laughing*]: He won't be able to see an elephant's ass, jus' *look!*

SILVA: *Shhh!*

[*Archie Lee has staggered onto the porch with shotgun. He collides with a column then shoots wildly at a shadow swaying in the wind. Aunt Rose screams. Archie Lee falls off the porch.*]

ARCHIE: WOP, WOP, YELLA-BELLY, WHERE ARE YUH?

[*He careens dizzily around the yard, fires at a chicken coop, then into the wheelless and topless chassis of the derelict automobile, then here, then there. He exits around the side of the house.*]

BABY DOLL: How long we gonna be possums up this tree?

SILVA: Shhh! Police will be here soon.

[*The wind is loud, shadows are swaying crazily in the yard. Aunt Rose scuttles out of the front door onto the porch, weighed down by her ancient suitcase, roped together. We hear the shotgun again.*]

AUNT ROSE: E-E-EEE! Baby Doll, honey? Baby Doll, honey?

SILVA: Don't answer yet!

[*THERE IS A SHOTGUN BLAST FROM THE BACK OF THE HOUSE.*]

AUNT ROSE: Terrible thunder-stawm's struck! Heaven have mercy, I hope it's not a cyclone!

[*She drops her suitcase, backs against wall, hand to her thin chest. Sound: fade in police siren approaching. Light: circular and blue pattern of the police car light behind the house. Archie Lee screams: "Baby Doll! Baby Doll!"*]

BABY DOLL: Poor ol' Aunt Rose Comfort, she don't know where to go or what to do.

217

SILVA: Does anyone know where to go or what to do, *Bambina?*

[*He draws her tight into his arms.*

[*Archie stumbles maniacally into view.*]

ARCHIE: Baby Doll, my baby! Yella son of a—

[*He staggers over a crate and sprawls onto ground among the litter of uncollected garbage. The police appear and pick him up.*]

Wha's this, who's you?

SHERIFF: This here is Sheriff Coglan and that there's Deputy Tufts, Archie Lee, and right around here is the wagon. Got a call on you, boy!

[*They support his limping figure upstage.*]

ARCHIE: Is something wrong, what is it, what're you doin'?

SHERIFF: Takin' you into town, boy.

ARCHIE: Not without my Baby Doll, not without my baby! BABY DOLL!

DEPUTY: Hell, she don't need you, she don't need nobody tonight. Ha Ha!

[*They disappear back of the house. A motor starts, then rapidly fades out.*]

AUNT ROSE [*in a tremulous voice*]: "Rock of ages, cleft for me,
Let me hide myself in thee!"

[*Night sounds—musical, peaceful. Aunt Rose rocks on the front porch and sings. The lovers remain in the tree as the lights fade to a single blue light on the lovers that eventually goes out as if the moon passed behind a cloud.*]

END OF PLAY

The following is the lyric for Ruby to sing at the beginning of
Act II, Scene 2:

RUBY [*singing and moving sensually*]:

> Many white gents respected high
> are respected higher when they die.
> Oh, we miss 'em but we know
> they gone to where white gents all go.
>
> Maybe so and maybe no
> but when I turn the red lights low
> and when I turn the music slow,
> a doubt will creep into my mind,
>
> a wonder that I can't deny,
> would they ruther climb the sky
> than the stairs at Ruby's place
> with girls in satin underlace!?
>
> Brown satin girls, dressed in lace,
> —at Ruby's place.